NIGHTS
OF THE
CREAKING BED

By The Same Author:

The Carnivorous City

NIGHTS
OF THE
CREAKING BED

Toni Kan

Abuja - London

First published in 2019 by Cassava Republic Press

Abuja – London

Copyright ©Toni Kan 2008

A CIP catalogue record for this book is available from the National Library of Nigeria and the British Library.

ISBN 978-1-911115-84-7

eISBN 978-1-911115-85-4

Book design by Tobi Ajiboye

Cover & Art Direction by Seyi Adegoke

Printed and bound in Great Britain by Bell and Bain Ltd., Glasgow

Distributed in Nigeria by Yellow Danfo

Distributed in the UK by Central Books Ltd.

Distributed in the US by Consortium Books

Stay up to date with the latest books, special offers and
exclusive content with our monthly newsletter.
Sign up on our website:
www.cassavarepublic.biz
Twitter: @cassavarepublic
Instagram: @cassavarepublicpress
Facebook: facebook.com/CassavaRepublic
Hashtag: #CreakingBed #ReadCassava

For **PJ**; for the years past and the years to come

Table of Contents

Strangers

Nobody saw them arrive.

But everyone knew when they left; none of us on that street will forget even if we lived to be hundred.

They were two young boys on the cusps of manhood. Nineteen? Twenty? Twenty-one? Who knew and who really cared. They were strangers, not one of us, so nobody poked their nose into their business.

All we knew is that we woke up one morning and they were there; a tall, thin one and a fat round one. Sam and Silas they said their names were.

They appeared as if out of nowhere and occupied that house, the empty one right next to the shoemakers. They cleaned out one room, and moved in. No one asked questions. In many ways, it seemed as if we welcomed warmth in that house, as if the flicker of the candle they lit at night sent a warm glow right down the street. Gloom must have made us sentimental.

They didn't go to work like we did. In the mornings they would walk down the street, washing cars that had been parked outside their compounds. Grateful owners dropped naira notes in appreciation and sometimes if they saw a woman walking home laden with shopping, they would run after her and offer a hand in exchange for a tip, a fruit, a loaf of bread, something earned.

Three months ago, when the lawyer moved into your former flat, they helped wash it down. They helped paint it and they helped him reconnect loose wires. Those two, Sam and Silas, there was nothing they couldn't do.

Where did they come from, you ask again? No one knew. I tell you, we woke up one morning and they were there; a tall thin one and a fat round one.

They didn't seem to ever leave that street in the eight months they were with us. I saw them every morning when I stepped out on the balcony for my morning smoke, washing a car or sitting out on the steps that led into the house they occupied and sunning themselves like well-fed lizards.

'Good morning, bros,' they would call, and I would wave.

Sometimes, the thin one, the more friendly and loquacious one, would put two fingers to his lips and send out imaginary smoke rings. It was his way of bumming a cigarette off me.

If I was in a good mood or had a full pack, I would signal to him and he would come over and receive two sticks for himself and his friend. Most times I just ignored him and he would smile and hail me.

'The Big Bros!'

They washed my car too. At first, on days when I came back too late and too drunk to manoeuvre into my spot in the compound, but in time they took to coming into the compounds to wash the cars especially for those of us who didn't have drivers or security men to do it for us.

Did anyone mind? No. We did not mind. Why should we? They were happy to get a hundred naira, two hundred naira, and we were happy to give it; one tenth of what we would pay at the car wash.

And they could wash cars, those boys.

'We dey mix Omo with kerosene,' Sam, the thin, tall one told me when I commended them one morning.

'Na the *combinate* dey make am shine,' he explained.

The combinate, I muttered under my breath as I fished out a two hundred naira note.

'The Big Bros,' he hailed as he picked up his bucket, his plump friend waddling out behind him.

The fat one was always silent and always reading.

What did he read? I don't know. I never bothered to check but he always had a book or something; some tattered paperback or heavy tome, filched out of some dump or maybe bought second-hand.

They were strangers and strangers have strange ways. That was what everyone thought and said. But did it stop us from sending them on errands? No. Neither did it stop us from watching them dig and shovel out dirt from our gutters on the last Saturday of every month when the whole street turned out for the monthly environmental sanitation exercise.

We would all stand or sit, reading newspapers and talking politics, Baba Mercy's voice echoing, while the two boys dug and shovelled, raking out muck and grime.

And when they were done, we would say well done, well done and scurry off into our compounds.

They were hard workers those boys. Nothing was too tough or too menial.

Last month, just before what happened happened, they even joined the masons when Baba Mercy decided to complete roofing and plastering the house he abandoned after his daughter died.

I watched them work, hefting bags of cement onto strong shoulders and then running up the scaffold with pans laden with concrete as if it was cotton fluff. There was something about them, the rippling muscles under taut skin for Sam and the folds of flesh that wobbled on Silas, that spoke of purpose and youth, and something indiscernible.

Many of us wanted our brothers who lived with us to be like them. We wanted our siblings to work, to have purpose, to be engaged instead of sitting all day at home watching cable TV, playing computer games and chasing after the girls like dogs.

Did any girls visit them? Of course! People talked, said they were munching through the house girls on the streets like soft bread. Especially that Sam. He had a mouth on him. It was easy for him to charm the pants and ragged wrappers off the house helps. I used to see him at work. He was a maestro, reminded me all the time of you back then in school, when you were king, before you found Christ or was it the other way round?

I should leave Christ alone. Is that how you are going to save my soul? Ok, I have left him alone.

Sam had a quick retort for everything and he laughed like he owned the street. The laughter is what I remember the most because it was silent later that day. His laughter was loud, and care-free, like a rumble of thunder rolling through the heavens.

You remember what you told me back then at Jos, in school; that to get a babe you must abandon shame. That was Sam. The way he went at the girls, you could see that this was a man in whose vocabulary the word shame did not exist.

Soon, some of the street girls began to get curious. We heard things too. There were warnings. The boys who lived on the street, who did not want to see these strangers dip their fingers into their pots, sent out warnings. They accosted Sam and Silas in their den at night. Threats were made.

Sam and Silas withdrew. They still washed cars, they still helped women laden with shopping, they still raked out grime from our gutters but now they did it as if in slow motion. They had been told who they were, what they were- strangers! They didn't belong. They were there because we allowed them. They would do well to stand on one foot, play the cock on new territory, to not get too familiar.

But it did not last. Two days, three days, one week, and they were back to their jolly selves. Sam's laughter cleaved the air, waking up the somnolent afternoons. They re-joined the street boys where they played football at the corner. They bummed cigarettes off those of us who smoked. They danced on the streets, winked at the girls and lived. They were boys after all and that was what boys did. Boys think they are invincible, that they are above it all. They think they can stare death in the face and laugh it to scorn.

We accepted them again, but still like we had before, as strangers, with suspicion in our eyes, always with unspoken questions: where did they come from, what did they want.

The balance of things seemed restored and we saw them and yet did not see them. They were Sam and Silas, the thin one and the fat one and then something happened.

I was away for a few days. Where did I go? Awka, Audit duty. A branch was sending in funny reports.

There was not much going on but foolishness. A young boy, newly Chartered, First Class from Ife, saddled with a job too big for him. He was fumbling, making mistakes.

He was a good boy. I liked him. We shared drinks on quiet

lonely evenings at the bar of the hotel where I stayed. He smoked too, so we bonded over Dorchester cigarettes and tepid beer. He was eager to please and buy drinks as provincials often are when they see someone from the Head Office. I did not think it was because he wanted to sway me. He had done nothing wrong, nothing criminal, really, just made mistakes that misrepresented things.

I paid for the drinks instead. I bought him drinks night after night because I was sorry. I pitied him. His job was toast. Once I sent in my report, they would fire him. That's how banks work. We need to get it right, all the time, or people lose money and if people lose money, we lose money and if we lose money, we lose everything.

So, we spent those nights drinking beer and smoking and talking about Lagos and comparing Awka girls to Lagos girls with their over-eager ways.

'You must open an account here before you go. I get customers plenty,' he said with a wink, as he implored me to pick a girl, any girl that caught my eye from the bevy he presented.

Did they fire him after I sent in my report? Yes. He is gone now. And no, we did not keep in touch.

So, I came back and there was no Sam and there was no Silas.

The street seemed strangely quiet like someone had stolen its soul, ripped it off like some cheap carpet.

'Where are those boys?' I asked my neighbour's wife the next morning.

'Which boys?' she asked and there was something in her tone, a glint in her eyes that looked like shame, or was it guilt?

'Sam and Silas, the boys that live in that house,' I said, pointing even though I did not need to. Everyone knew who they were and where they lived and once you said those boys, everyone knew who you were referring to.

'They left,' she said and hurried off.

It was strange, I thought. They had settled in. Why would they leave now without farewell to the Big Bros?

And so, I forgot about them like you would a stranger who bumps into you at the Mall. The briefest of encounters, it does not register for long.

But then they returned.

Yes, they did and now, I wish they hadn't. I wish they had read the auguries, seen the bile curdling to rage, smelled the scent of blood hovering in the afternoon air.

They were quieter now, withdrawn, tentative. They washed few cars, did not beg for cigarettes and they lazed more, not just like well-fed lizards but lazy ones.

'Where did you people go?' I asked the morning I saw them washing my car.

Sam did not speak, instead he scrubbed harder, the soap suds foaming white as he went at my tyre as if the tyre posed some mortal danger.

'Where did you people go?' I repeated, convinced now that something had gone wrong while I was away.

'Cell,' Silas said.

'Cell?'

'Dem lock us up,' he said his voice low, eyes lowered.

'Who lock una up?'

'Baba Mercy,' Sam said now, standing straight, his face contorted in rage and shame and what I suppose was fear too.

'Nothing wey we do. Somebody steal tyre. Dem say na we. Dem search our room. Nothing. If we steal tyre where we go hide am? How we go sell am. We no dey comot for dis street. I tell dem, check Baba Mercy house, dat 'im son, Clement, na 'im dey do dat kind thing. Baba Mercy vex. Clement vex. Dem say we be thief. Dem beat us. Dem call police. Dem carry us go police. Six days, The Big Bros. Six days, we dey for cell. And nothing wey we do dem. We come back, our TV don go. Dem piss for our room. Shit for our bed. Wetin we do?'

He was crying now, the brush slipping from his hand.

I watched him struggle to pick it up. The bravado was gone, the youthful invincibility shorn off. This broken person before me was a boy and he was confused. The real world had confronted him with its harsh realities and he was muddled. They thought they had built a home but it was a shack really, some flimsy, ramshackle thing. It was no more than Terra lacking firma.

I said sorry. I gave them my card. I said if anything like that happens again, you call me.

'That is my number. My brother is a lawyer.'

You ask whether that's all I did? Yes, that's all I did. What more could I do? Go to Baba Mercy and ask him why? Question a landlord because of two strangers? We live here and they are squatters. We stick with our own. Would I believe a stranger's story over yours?

But I wish now that I had done more, maybe asked them to leave, scared them off instead of showing empathy because if I had, what happened would never have happened.

You ask me what happened? But you know, you read it in the papers. Oh, you want to know what really, really happened?

Ok, it was a Saturday. I was home. I hadn't been feeling well so I hadn't gone out on the balcony to smoke. So, I didn't see them that morning.

I woke. I made tea, laced it with ginger and lime and just lay there in the dark, curtains drawn, listening to the BBC.

It was the screaming that woke me up, the cries. I pulled on my shirt and went to the balcony. Sam and Silas were already bleeding, shirts torn, eyes swollen.

I raced downstairs.

'Wetin happen?' I cried, pushing at the crowd. They were thirsty for blood, that crowd; a baying mob with bared teeth.

They had them on the floor now. They were kneeling in the dirt. Silas was quiet. Eyes cast down, lips moving like he was mumbling something. A prayer, maybe, or words from something he had read somewhere.

'What happened?' I asked, staring from angry face to angry face, now that I was within the perimeter of blood.

'Dem say two pikin dey miss. Dem say we steal dem.' Silas said as a kick sent him into the puddle, spattering me with dirty water.

Clement had a stick as he towered over them. He lashed out at one and then the other, drawing blood, their screams echoing.

I looked up; men and women stood up there, on their balconies watching the orgy of blood. They all said nothing, did nothing, complicit in their silence. What were the boys after all but strangers? What were they doing here if not to steal and kidnap children?

'Clement, wait,' I said staying his blow by grabbing his stick.

His eyes were red. This was not about the missing children. This was about the accusation. This was a young man marking his turf with blood.

'Broda Sylvester, leave my stick,' he snarled.

But I held on. Staring into his eyes, searching for that boy, the one I gifted my shirts to. The one I gave my old shoes. The one that said he wanted to marry my younger sister. He wasn't there. This was a monster. A man made mad by his grudge. He would not be appeased, except by blood.

'Clement, hold on.' I said.

There was a flickcr, as if of recognition, then the veil descended again. He tugged at the stick, ripped a bloody gash through my palm and began to lash out at the two boys, drawing blood and screams as if my intervention had intensified his rage, incensed him beyond reason.

I held my bleeding palm, as I looked from one to the other. Faces blurred into each other.

'Where una hide the pikin?' Angry voices demanded but no one waited for an answer. The boys were guilty by virtue of who they were. Strangers.

'Make una bring tyre. Somebody bring tyre.'

I pushed through the crowd. I needed my phone. I needed to call the police. I raced into my compound. The gate to the staircase that led upstairs was locked. Someone had banged it shut. I tugged at it, leaving a bloody smear on the door handle. It didn't give.

I was bleeding, the redness congealing on the hairs at the back of my hand.

I knocked on my neighbours' doors. Their doors were locked. No one answered.

I raced out of the compound again to the shoemaker. Surely he would help. They sat with him all day. They were neighbours.

I found him, hunched over and sobbing, a broken old man.

'Give me your phone. Give me your phone.'

I dialed 767, the Lagos state emergency number.

'Good morning. What's your emergency?'

'Please get me the police. Please. They are killing two boys on my street.'

'Where is your street?' she asked and I told her.

'Please hurry. They are going to burn them alive.'

The crowd was huge now, so huge and so alive that I couldn't reach the centre. Someone had found a tyre, it seemed. Someone had brought petrol. They had been doused in it and Sam was begging, his voice raised, plaintive, fighting for their lives. Silas was silent as usual and even though I could not see, I could imagine his lips moving wordlessly as someone struck the match.

People staggered back as a collective cry went up all over the street. Men tripped over men as they scattered. And now I had them in my view. The fire was hungry. Licking at them, blinding them, mixing flesh and textile in an ugly alchemy.

Then, suddenly, I saw Sam turn then run straight at Clement. Taking him by surprise, he knocked Clement down, fell on top of him and enfolded him in a fiery embrace. Clement did not stand a chance.

By the time the police arrived, there were three charred bodies and a quiet street. Their blood thirst sated, my neighbours had skulked indoors.

I was the only one outside when the police arrived. I gave them names. I pointed to houses. I knocked on doors. I watched men taken away, neighbours I had lived with for six years. Eyes glared at me but I did not care.

Upstairs, I held my throbbing hand with the caked blood and wept for those two. I knew I was done with that street. I knew the street was done with me too, so after I cleaned my gash, I began to pack.

And I was still packing when I heard the screaming.

Someone had found the missing kids; unconscious but safe in the back of a broken-down bus where they had gone in to play.

The Passion of Pololo

Pololo walks into his room and stops dead in his tracks, the
tennis racquet slipping from his grip.

His mother is lying naked in his bed and atop her is a naked
young man.

'Mo... mo!' he tries to speak but the word will not be formed.
Like an angler's hook stuck in a fish, it will not yield easily.

His mother has scrambled off the bed now and what he
remembers years and years later is the image of his beautiful
mother, naked breasts heaving, one hand outstretched in a
plea, a finger on her lips urging silence.

Pololo stares, unable to articulate the words that want to
burst out, unable to mouth the word he loves the most. He
cannot say "Mother" because the word is marooned. Pololo
has begun to stutter.

They hear the knock and stiffen. Pololo stares at them, stares
at their eyes widening into scared orbs in their faces, guilty
faces beaded with anxious sweat.

'Paul, is your mum there?' his father asks. But Paul does not
answer, cannot answer.

'Yes, darling,' his mother says, her eyes begging him to be
silent.

Paul hears, rather than sees, the swish of a silk robe and then
his mother is stepping out and he is standing there, leaning on

the wall and looking at the scared young man, the one who lives next door with his brother, the one Pololo calls Uncle Mike, the one who is studying medicine at the university, the one who has been teaching him how to drive.

They stare at each other and as the young man's face blurs through the haze of tears that films Pololo's eyes, he can hear his mother's trilling laughter as she asks his father why they are back so early.

'My friends didn't turn up, so I played just one set with Dr. Osondu. You know he's not feeling so well,' he tells her.

'Come to the bathroom, I'll run you a bath.'

'You must join me,' his father says and his mother's shy giggle is a knife twisting in Pololo's gut.

The young man can hear, too, and when the sounds die and they both know it is safe to leave, the young man scrambles into his clothes and, opening the door a crack and peering out, flees the house, leaving his sandals behind. From now on, each time Pololo awakes, the oversize sandals are lying there, screaming at him like an insistent cry.

She smothers him with affection. Guilt is a sturdy tree, with fragile branches that droop with tenderness. He knows. She knows. And by his silence, he has become complicit. It is them, now, against his father. The young man is a faint footnote on a forgotten page of their sad story. But there are things that are more difficult to forget, images that will never go away, heaving breasts that will never age, or sag, or droop.

His father is surprised at his stutter.

'Don't joke with something like that Paul. It could become a habit, you know,' his father says.

His father insists on calling him Paul, his given name. Every other person calls him Pololo, the pet name he unwittingly gave himself when, as a four year old, he had first tried to write his name.

A psychiatric doctor, his father is always polite. He treats everyone like a mentally-ill patient. His words are soft, cushioned to avoid giving offence. His voice is always low, modulated so that it does not startle. Pololo watches his father across the dining table. He wants to tell him that this is not a joke. He wants to say, 'My tongue is fettered by a secret I cannot utter.' He wants to open his mouth and scream and yell and lay bare his mother's shame. But he cannot. The image that rears up in his head will not let him. He watches his very intelligent father and wonders how he can be so blind.

Back at school after the break, his friends laugh when he tries to speak and the words will not bud. 'Po..po..po..lo..lo!' they jeer and laugh.

He is thirteen now and, like his friends, has discovered sex. At night, they sneak out of the dorm and head to the bathrooms. They leaf through the pages of a skin magazine and then, lined up against the wall, pleasure themselves until the white tiles are slimy with semen.

When they are caught, the principal sends for their parents. His father is away on a course, so his mother comes instead.

In the principal's office, his mother cries and Pololo knows that the tears are not on his account. She weeps for herself. Guilt has her impaled on a stake.

'They are young men, we know, and they are growing,' the principal is saying. 'But if we let this pass, they will corrupt the whole school and we don't want that to happen.'

The punishment is twelve strokes of the cane at the assembly hall and a letter of undertaking from the parents that their children will be of good behaviour, failing which they will be expelled.

His mother signs the letter and as he walks her to her car, she keeps dabbing at her eyes with her handkerchief. When they get to her car, she looks up at him. Her eyes are puffy and swimming in tears.

'Please forgive me.' These are the only words she says.

The next Monday, when he steps forward to receive his punishment, Pololo survives the ordeal by focusing on the image that threatens to blind him, the image that will not go away.

After the bathroom debacle, his mother comes to visit him every Sunday. After church, she drives the forty kilometres to his all-boys school. They sit, swaddled in silence, in her car, while he nibbles at the food she has brought him. Pololo doesn't feel like eating, never feels like eating any more, so he saves the food and when it is time for his mother to leave, he takes the food flask and goes to his friends who are waiting.

'Man, your mother is beautiful,' they always say.

And each time, Pololo stops himself from saying, 'You should see her naked.'

And that is the image that torments him, the ghost that haunts him. The only thing he saw when he looked in those skin magazines and cradled himself in his palms: *naked breasts heaving, one hand outstretched in a plea, a finger on her lips urging silence.*

Home on holiday from his first semester at the university, Pololo is awoken by a searing pain in his abdomen and upper back. He cannot sleep. He gulps down a cup of cold water and doubles over with pain. Fighting the pain without success, he knocks on his parents' door.

They drive him to the hospital. It is cold. The harmattan wind is howling and his father has the windows wound all the way up.

'Easy, Paul,' his father says every time Pololo sighs or groans.

His mother is sitting behind and each time his father says 'easy', she strokes Pololo's clean shaven head and mutters a prayer. Oppressed by the weight of the burden she bears, his mother has found refuge in the church and in prayers, but the touch of her hand sires goose pimples on his skin.

The doctor is a family friend and lives at the back of his huge clinic. Pololo is lying on the couch when he enters in his pyjamas.

'Hello Dan, Bettina. Long time. Now, what is the problem, young man?'

Pololo tells him about the pain and the doctor unbuttons his shirt and presses down on his upper abdomen.

'Here? You feel anything?'

Pololo nods. The doctor presses further down and Pololo shakes his head.

'And your back?'

'Yes, here,' Pololo tells him, lifting off the couch to show him where.

'Has this happened before?'

'Yes. In school, but it wasn't this bad.'

The doctor moves from the couch to settle behind his huge table and pulls on his glasses. He flips open the family casebook a nurse has brought in and begins to write.

'You drink beer?' he asks and Pololo nods. 'You smoke?'

'No.'

'I think you have an ulcer and I am surprised. Does it run in the family, Dan?' Pololo's father shakes his head.

'So where is this from, young man? What are you thinking

about? Girls, eh? You know they say you don't get an ulcer from what you eat, but from what's eating you. So what's eating you, young man?'

Pololo smiles and says, 'I don't know, doctor.'

'We will manage it and see how it goes. If it comes back, you have to let me know. But the alcohol has to go for now, okay?'

'Yes, doctor,' he says, getting off the couch.

'And you shouldn't let things bother you too much. You are too young to have an ulcer. Think of all the beer you will be missing, eh?'

Pololo gets a jab for the pains and collects his drugs from the nurse and they drive home in silence.

He sits at the back, thinking about the doctor's daughter. He has known Isabel since kindergarten where everyone used to ask whether she was his sister. They all said she looked like his mother and, a young lady now, she looks exactly the way his mother looked in pictures taken when she was their age.

He didn't see much of Isabel during secondary school except when the two families met at church or social gatherings, but once they met again on campus they had become lovers, and friends going through his picture album always mistook his mother for Isabel's mother.

The first night they made love, his first time ever, Pololo had screamed out "Mother" and from that moment his tongue was loosened and he would never stutter again.

There were other girls after Isabel. But all the girls looked alike. It was as if he was replicating Isabel. They were all tall, dark, curvaceous and with big eyeballs. Just like Isabel, just like his mother.

But whatever he sought in the string of girls who graced his bed remained just outside his grasp. He was like an adventurer seeking something that was always a step ahead of him. He knew what it was but could not fathom how to lay hold of it. But he knew that some day, his sojourn would lead him to that which he sought.

His father is on a course and Pololo is home on vacation and alone with his mother when his fever overwhelms him. Through with dinner, she tells him to turn off the oven in five minutes while she takes a shower, or else she will be late for church.

When Pololo pushes the door open, his mother has one leg on the stool by the dressing mirror. She is naked and cupped in her left palm is the cream she is applying to her skin.

He is naked, too, and the distance that yawns between them is a space filled with sad memories.

She stands still and watches her son with eyes hooded with shame and sadness, while her shoulders droop with pain and a burden that will not go away. She watches her dear son, his head bent, his intent clear, but she will not bridge that gap. She will not give him that which he seeks. She will not trade one sin for another. He must take that which he desires by force and against her will.

Eternity is compressed into that moment when the past mates with the present and leaves the future stillborn with time enough for just one dream.

She hears the door close and then she sits on the bed and cries for the son she has lost.

My Perfect Life

'Sylvia, this is madness, o! You know, this is madness. You are pouring hot embers into your own wrapper. What makes you think it won't get burnt?'

Auntie Bibi was right. I was indeed playing with fire and I didn't see how I was not going to get burnt but I was also, on the other hand, feeling the kind of tingling aliveness I had not felt for a very long time. The way I felt, it was as if I had been asleep for twenty years and then someone had knocked and woken me up and, instead of lethargic drowsiness, I was feeling rejuvenated and alive.

It was a Saturday and, like most women I know in Lagos, I had just finished my shopping for the month at The Palms. I had made my second and last trip to the car and was almost leaving when my eyes went to the message my husband had scribbled for me on the stick-on pad he had stuck on the dashboard of my car.

'Don't forget my roll-on, o!'

Now, I am not trying to blame anybody for what Auntie Bibi called my "moral capitulation" but believe me, if my husband had not asked me to buy him his roll-on deodorant, I would have gone home and nothing would have happened and my life would have been one happy joyride.

But he did and when I saw the message, I turned off the

engine, stepped out of the car and walked back into the mall. And that was where I met this person from my past who swept through me like a hurricane, and wrecked my simple and well-ordered life.

The last time I saw Seun, I was twenty years old and in my first year at the College of Education. He was the first man I fell in love with, the first man to, as we used to say in those days, see my nakedness.

How did we meet? I had been going home for the Christmas break and Seun had offered me a ride from Abraka to Warri. Alone, I would never have met him because I never, ever, accepted rides from strangers. But I was in the company of two other colleagues, Cynthia and Greg, and Seun happened to be Greg's brother's friend.

Seun insisted on dropping me off at home and coming to see me the next evening. I spent three weeks at home and Seun was a constant presence, visiting me every evening. By the end of the first week, my parents and siblings were all enamoured of Seun who used to bring the house down with his humour and jokes.

When it was time to go back to school in January, Seun took me shopping and filled up the boot of his car, as well as my box, with provisions, cosmetics, goodies and clothes. I was the envy of my friends as we spent close to thirty minutes offloading all the stuff he had bought me.

'I want to marry you,' Seun said to me later that evening, as we sat inside his car and kissed.

'Bush man, is that how people propose in your village?' I asked, laughing.

'This is Abraka. My village is Sagamu, in Ogun state.'

'I know, Our Man from Sagamu,' I said, mimicking my father,

who wouldn't stop calling Seun "Our Man from Sagamu" in reference to a paperback he had in his library.

'I am serious. I have to go and see your parents officially when you come home for Easter. I will let my people know.' I didn't say a word. I just sat there and watched him talk.

We had known each other for all of three weeks and even though we had not gone beyond kissing and his feverish fingers teasing my inner thighs, he was already talking marriage. What else could a woman ask for?

Seun came to see me every weekend, driving from Warri after work on Friday and leaving late on Sunday and it was on one of those weekly visits that we finally made love.

We had been dating for two months or so and that Friday night, after he had eaten and was set to go back to his guest house, I told him I would go with him.

'Why?' he asked and I felt the rising flush of anger.

'Why? Is someone waiting for you at the guest house?' I asked and it was his turn to get angry.

'What kind of question is that?'

'I am sorry,' I began, placing a conciliatory arm on his thigh. 'It's just that I thought we should spend the night together. Every time you leave me, I am not myself. I can't sleep because I keep thinking about you. And you know, it's my safe period,' I said, smiling up at him.

'Are you sure you want to come with me?' he asked, cupping my face in his palms.

'Yes.'

'You have to be sure, Sylvia. I am here for marriage not a fling, so I am ready to wait...' I placed a finger on his lips to silence him.

'I am ready, so shut up and let's go.'

I know it's a crazy thing to say, but I wish Seun was the first man for every woman, because he was born to give pleasure. The first time we made love was over two decades ago, but that day when I saw Seun at The Palms, I felt myself go wet and weak in the knees as I remembered that first night, how he had undressed me slowly and then kissed me all the way from my feet to my lips, stopping intermittently to pleasure my hard nipples.

I remembered now how loud I'd screamed and then began trembling when he buried his face between my legs and brought me to a toe-curling, scream-inducing orgasm. I remember screaming so loud that Seun had got scared and stopped, refusing to finish what he had started until the next morning.

I still remember how much pleasure Seun gave me that morning when we finally went the whole way and he brought me to climax after climax.

Sex with Seun was an addiction and once we'd started, I finally understood why he had been asking me to wait. I just couldn't get enough and I remember how I used to lie in bed at night dreaming wild dreams and waiting feverishly for Friday; and I remember the Friday he didn't come how I almost died.

I loved Seun. He was kind, gentle and in tune with me. I also loved being intimate with him, something my older friends said was a good mix. So, you can imagine how I looked forward to Easter when he would come to officially ask for my hand.

But you know what Ola Rotimi said: joy has a slender back that breaks too soon.

When I told my father that Seun had proposed and was coming with his people to see him, he cocked an eyebrow and said: 'I thought you two were just playing, o! My first daughter cannot marry a Yoruba man. No way! Do you know what Yoruba people did to my uncle after the war? Never!'

My father's words were dangerous winds that knocked me senseless and I thought I would die. But of course I didn't. I was alive, above ground and hurting like hell. Those who say heartache is a fable are mad. Heartache is a killer. It drains you and saps you of energy and the will to live. It turns your days into a living hell and leaves you overcast with gloom. I wouldn't have felt the kind of pain I felt even if my father had picked up a cutlass and chopped off my arm. At least then I would have only felt pain until the doctors did their bit. But with heartache, there is no cure. You ache and ache and ache, with nothing to ease your pain or ameliorate your hurt.

'Defy your father and marry me,' Seun begged me one Saturday night, when I had defied my father's warning to stop seeing him.

We had just finished making feverish love, our first time in over a month, and were basking in the heady afterglow. 'You know I can't,' I said.

'Why can't you?' he asked, getting up and sitting cross- legged on the bed, his flaccid manhood dangling between his feet.

'My father will kill me,' I said, reaching out to touch his manhood, but he slapped my hand off.

'This is serious,' he said with a stern look as he covered his nakedness with a pillow.

'So you really think he will kill you?' Seun asked and I nodded.

'You don't know my father. He can be loving and playful, but you don't want to know what he can do when you cross him.'

'Well, what if he can't find you?' Seun asked, favouring me with a funny look.

'What do you mean?'

'What if you defy your father, then still go on with your life because he can't touch you?' Seun asked, staring intently now and leaving me with a strange feeling.

'I don't understand. How can I go on with my life without my father touching me?' I asked, and then he said the scariest thing you could tell a young girl who was not even twenty yet:

'Let's elope. You know, run so far away they will never find us. We can start a new life.' But I was shaking my head and muttering 'No, no, no' under my breath. But the more I shook my head, the faster he spoke as if we were in a heated competition to see who would win.

'We can go to America or the UK. I told you I was planning to leave this country before I met you. We can go there. I have friends and brothers. We won't lack where to stay. I can get you a visa. Please, let's get so far away they won't see us. Your father will miss you but after a few years, by the time you send back pictures of our children, his grandchildren, the man will come round. Please, let's go,' he begged, taking my hands and looking up into my tear-filled eyes.

'I can't run away, Seun. I just can't. I will die. Please, think of something else. Something that will make sense, something I can do and not go mad. Please.'

I cried so hard that when I got home, I had a blinding headache that turned into a migraine and then blasted malaria that led to a four night stay at the hospital. It was on the third day that I realised what was ailing me. It wasn't malaria and it wasn't migraine. It was heartache. The words Seun spoke as I stepped out of his house had reverberated so loudly they left me sick.

'I love you Sylvia but I can't wait. I am leaving Nigeria for good.'

Those words were like sharp knives digging into my heart and making it bleed and, if I thought I had suffered while I was in the hospital, nothing prepared me for what I would get into when I left the hospital and came home.

As soon as my father, who brought me home, retired to his bedroom, I stole out of the house through the back door and ran all the way to the bus stop before getting on a bus that took me to Seun's house.

He wasn't home. The house was locked and there was no sign of his car. After waiting until it was dark, I resolved to go and see him at his office on Monday. I got to the office and was told that Seun was on leave and wouldn't be back for two more weeks.

To say that I was devastated would be to put it mildly. I didn't have a clue what to do. I still don't know how I managed to rise and walk out of that office and find my way home.

Back home, I moped, my mind full of desperate thoughts. I remembered how we met, his tentative questions, how he kept staring at me in the rear view mirror and the way he always managed to change the conversation so that he could dwell on me. I remembered his deep laughter and the jokes he told. I remembered my screams and the tears of joy and pleasure I shed after I climaxed that first time.

When Seun didn't show up at work after two weeks, I realised with certainty that I had lost him and that my life would never be the same again.

They say time heals but what they never say is that time is a bad healer. It leaves hideous scars. I had those scars, and the thing most people don't know about scars is that they are masks. They disguise things, covering up things that bleed and fester.

'Sylvia?'
The voice was low, deep and tentative and I almost did not

turn. It sounded like a young man calling out a woman's name and not being sure whether the lady is who he thinks she is. I had known such timid, unsure men as a young woman and I couldn't think of who could be calling me. So, I kept walking, but the caller must have noticed my slight hesitation, the pause that was no longer than a heartbeat and so he followed me outside and called me again.

This time, I stopped and turned. A man was standing about two metres away from me. He was tall, dark and handsome in a greying, mature way. He was dressed casually, in brown chinos and a blue tee shirt.

'Sylvia,' he said again and this time there was no question mark behind the name. His voice was saying, 'So, it's really you!' and I stared, unsure of who he was or what he expected me to say.

Then, as he approached, something clicked in my brain and I began to peel off the cloak the years had garbed him in: the grey hairs, the wrinkles, the crows' feet around the smiling eyes. The man standing before me with a smile crinkling his eyes, was no other than my darling Seun, the first man I had ever loved and whom, I realised with a jolt as I dropped my bag and rushed into his arms, I had never stopped loving.

He hugged me tightly until my ribs ached. Then he was holding me away from his body, his eyes probing my face, trying to see what the years had done to me.

'My God, you're still an incredibly beautiful woman,' he said.

'The years have been kind to you, too,' I said, appraising him with my eyes. Then, as his gaze dropped to my wedding finger, I said conversationally, 'I thought you were abroad.'

'I thought you were waiting for me,' he countered and I laughed, suddenly overwhelmed by a ripple of joy.

'Wait for you for twenty years? Do you know what you did to me when you disappeared without warning?' I said, remembering my heartache, yet surprised at how easily I warmed towards him, as if it hadn't been twenty years but a mere twenty days.

'I went to America,' he said and then paused. 'This is a long story and I think I should tell it sitting down. Come, I know a quiet place.'

Still not sure whether I was dreaming or actually awake, I walked beside Seun as he led me to a Discovery Jeep that smelled new. He pulled the door open for me, then walked round to the other side.

We drove out of The Palms and turned left towards the British International School. We made a right turn and then drove a short distance to the VI extension. Seun stopped in front of a huge gate and beeped the horn. The gate swung open and we drove in.

The house was a breathtaking one-storey affair. It sat alone in the middle of large grounds with paving stones. The landscaping was lush and the flowers were already in bloom.

'Welcome to Casa Seun.'

'This is your house?'

'Yes. I saw it two years ago on a visit and it took the owner nine months to agree to sell. It cost an arm and a leg but it is worth every penny. Let me give you the grand tour.' He led me from the foyer into the living room; then we passed through his study and exited into the kitchen which had been done up in black.

'It was white, but I changed it to black. Black has more character, don't you think?' he asked as he pulled open the refrigerator.

'More masculine, you mean?' I asked and he turned to me and smiled.

'You haven't changed. What shall it be? White wine or red?'

'Red,' I said, suddenly feeling exuberant and almost decadent.

Seun uncorked the bottle, poured, then handed me a glass.

'To love,' he said and I echoed him.

After he had shown me the guest room, which was almost a full house on its own, we continued the tour upstairs. There were four rooms upstairs and we entered the master bedroom through a well-equipped home gym.

'This is my retreat,' he said, waving his hand to take in the tastefully furnished bedroom and spilling some wine in the process.

'Easy,' I said, wondering whether he had been drinking before we met at The Palms.

'I'm drunk on joy,' he said, laughing as if he had read my thoughts. Then he set the glass and bottle down, reached out and took my glass and put it down, and then pulled me to him and kissed me.

I would be lying if I say I didn't expect it, if I say I didn't want it or that I hadn't been looking forward to him kissing me. I was curious to see whether it would be the same, whether his body would still melt into mine like it did twenty years before, whether my heart would still beat and flutter like it used to.

It did. My body tingled and caught fire as he kissed me and his hands went to my breast. I moaned as he found my nipple and tweaked. Then I let him carry me to his bed and kissed him back, hungrily, unashamedly, as he divested me and his finger found my wetness and stroked.

Seun and I made love that afternoon and once again I was a young woman, a virgin touched for the very first time and I was crying and screaming when he brought me to a shattering climax.

I fell asleep, lying in the crook of his arms. Time had ceased to matter, to make sense. I lay there, naked and without shame as if it was the most natural thing to do, sniffing his masculine scent, feeling his returning hardness against the soft flesh of my buttocks and feeling so incredibly alive all over.

And I would have lain there forever, waking up to make love to him like a desperately thirsty woman drinking from the cup of love he held up, if my phone had not begun to ring.

I reached into my handbag and dug it out. It was my husband.

I am forty-one years old. I am the wife of a kind, loving and gentle man. I am the mother of two children, a boy and a girl. I have a good job, live in a good home and I would say that I am happy and content.

So, why I am doing the crazy things I have been doing for weeks now? Why am I feeling deliriously happy and deliciously naughty? Why am I tingling all over and feeling wet in strange places? Why am I feeling so delinquent, like an eighteen-year-old who has just lost her virginity?

'Maybe it's a mid-life crisis,' I said to Auntie Bibi, trying to effect a serious demeanour but failing woefully as that smile, the kind my dead mother used to describe as the "I- know-something-you-don't-know smile," kept colouring my face bright.

'Mid-life what?' she asked and then launched into rapid fire Igbo. 'My people say 'why should I pity a big head when I have no plans of buying him or her a cap?' I don't know why I am still talking to you, but I'm sure it must be that fried rice I ate in your house two months ago. You've been such a naughty woman that I should be reaching for a whip to flog some sense into you.' Auntie Bibi started pacing around her office.

I watched her: her small, sure steps, the solid calves that appeared and disappeared as she moved, the serious black shoes she had on. I trailed her with my eyes: her regal bearing, her straight back, the black, polka-dotted silk dress, and I wondered how people could go through life so seriously, without a thought for the happiness that was possible if only they dared to look outside the shuttered windows of their lives, if only they tried to jump out of the constricting box of conformity fate had placed them inside. I looked from Auntie Bibi to the family portrait on her neat desk. She was seated with her husband and four children, two boys and two girls and wondered how people could live with such ordinariness, such strict compliance with things, such quotidian contentment with lives lacking in excitement.

Her husband's face was serious, the face of a barely literate but forward-looking Igbo man who had let his wife reach the pinnacle of educational excellence. I looked at her children, the boys with the fixed and determined stares of men who knew their purpose in life and the path to tread. I looked at her daughters, women who knew that a woman's life is one of duty and commitment to husband and family.

Auntie Bibi's face was the face of an intelligent woman who could let herself fly as high as she wanted to but who had, nevertheless, decided to clip her wings to make her husband and children happy.

My life had been trundling down the same path. I had been content to be a housewife, to go to work and return home to cook and clean and care for my family. I was happy to make love – no, have sex– once or twice a month, happy to just get by in that way of life until my time came. Until I met Seun again.

'You say your husband doesn't beat you, he doesn't womanise, and he doesn't have children outside. He provides well. Yet, you have been having sex with a stranger on a daily basis for the past how many days?' she said, her serious face bearing down on mine.

'Aunt Bibi, he is not a stranger. I've known him since...'

'Excuse me, my dear. A man you haven't seen for over thirty years is a stranger,' she snapped.

'I saw him last twenty years ago, not thir..' I began but she raised a hand and silenced me.

'Twenty or thirty. What is the difference, eh? What is the difference between where the baby comes from and where the shit comes from, eh? When a woman begins to behave the way you have done, people always ask how the husband treats her at home. Maybe he drove her into another man's arms because he didn't care for her enough. But you, there's no reason. Other than that you needed to scratch and keep scratching a stupid itch every woman learns to ignore.

'You think we don't want to do the same thing, too, to step out of our marriage and go wild? You think I don't want to do or haven't thought about doing that so many times I have lost count? But you think about your family, about what you have, what God has blessed you with and you say "Is this madness, this hunger, this lust" - because that's what it really is - "enough to make me jeopardise what I already have?" It is that thought that helps us keep our legs together, that makes us avert our eyes when other men ogle us, and go back home to our staid and boring husbands when men with fire in their loins are making us sweat with their wanton stares,' she said, then continued her pacing.

Sitting there watching her pace around the room, I was suddenly thankful and relieved. I was not a loose and useless woman, after all. I was actually normal, just like every other woman walking on the street, sitting at their boring desks in their dreary offices, lying inert under their hard-breathing husbands and feeling nothing where it matters.

All I had done differently was, instead of banishing the thoughts that had turned to cobwebs in my head the moment I hugged Seun that Saturday, I had let them bud. I had taken action. I had done something with them. That was all I had done.

And that evening as I went home, I was thanking Auntie Bibi in my heart. When Seun had asked me to leave my husband and children and follow him to America I had been too deliriously happy not to say yes. But when I got home and thought about it, it felt all wrong. They had done nothing to make me want to abandon them. So why should I deliberately hurt them?

'We lost a chance to be happy once. Let's not lose it again,' Seun had said. 'Let's go. Tell them you are travelling for another seminar or something. You went last year so no- one will raise eyebrows. Then tell them you won't come back when you get to the US.' He was bending to tickle my erect nipple with the tip of his tongue.

'They will be mad for a while, but they will get over it. But if you don't, they will be happy and you will be sad for ever.'
'You sound so American. Africans don't do such things,' I said with eyes clouded with tears.

'And that's because Africans pretend a lot. We never say what we mean, nor mean what we say.'

Seun leaves in a month's time. I have been seeing him and having sex with him almost every day since we met. My husband and kids do not suspect a thing. And why should they?

I have been a dutiful wife and doting mother all these years. The evening my husband called, I told him I was having car problems, and now I have taken leave at work so I can spend my days with Seun while my husband thinks I am carrying out research at The British Council.

Last night, Seun gave me back my international passport and there was a return ticket inside.

'Tell me you will come with me and I will confirm a seat for you immediately. I lost you once and I don't want to lose you again.'

I have my passport in my bag and I can picture life in America as Seun's wife in a big house where we'll make love every day. I can see long, languorous days at the beach and nights at the cinema or theatre. But I can also picture my husband, sad and grieving and my children cursing me in their hearts in a house that no longer knows laughter.

I have made my choice. The sound of my own laughter sounds better to my own ears.

The Harbinger

No one remembers now what he did before our fathers went to war.

All we remember is that he was the one who brought bad news. When his black, beat-up 504 trundled into a street in the barracks, all the children and women whose fathers and husbands had gone to war would shut their eyes and pray that his car did not sputter to a stop in front of their house.

He was the Harbinger.

I remember when he first arrived in the barracks. It was the day after I turned sixteen, two days after Meredith had let me deflower her as an early birthday present because she was set to go home for her grandfather's burial.

I remember because I'd gone to see Rita, who lived two houses away from Meredith. She had also promised to sleep with me as a belated birthday present. Her family would be at church, she said, and she had feigned malaria in order to stay at home.

I had just taken off my clothes and was fooling with Rita's bra strap when we heard the knock and froze.

'Jesus!' I said. 'You told me they went to Kingdom Hall.'

I got dressed fast and we crept to the living room.

'Who is there?' Rita called out, adjusting her blouse. She was shaking; my need was a distant memory.

'Hello, I just moved in and I want to borrow a hammer, if you have one.'

We sighed with relief as Rita opened the door and gave the man her father's hammer.

I studied him through an opening in the curtains. He was about five-ten, with a line of too-white teeth that contrasted with his dark face. He wore a green vest over camouflage shorts.

After shutting the door, Rita pointed to my open fly: 'Junior, your pingolo wants to cry.'

In my haste, I'd forgotten to pull on my boxers.

Rita and I laughed, relieved, but though she tried to coax me awake, I could never get up to do what I had come there for.

And that was how I first laid eyes on the Harbinger; he had moved into the house between Rita's and Meredith's.

He wasn't a priest or he would have worn a collar like the rest of them, but he was something important. Temisan, whose mother was an army nurse at the infirmary, said he was a doctor but didn't treat people with malaria or give injections. Instead, he looked into people's heads, especially soldiers with things in their heads

Whatever it was he did, we didn't take much notice of him until the war started.

I remember the night the war came into our home. My father returned from work with his shoulders slumped. I took his belt from him, the first thing he removed as he crossed the threshold. Then I stooped and waited for him to untie the laces of his military boots and hand them to me.

It was our ritual, as old as I could remember. Stooping with his belt, which was rough against the nape of my neck, I would wait for the two smells to mingle: the stale smell of alcohol on his breath and the rancidness of his stockinged feet as he pulled off the boots. The fusty aroma of those boots was one of the most reassuring smells of my childhood, one that I came to associate with fatherhood and manliness.

But there was something wrong that evening. There was no alcohol on his breath, and he didn't say, 'Thank you, Namesake,' as he always did when I picked up his boots.

I left the boots standing on their heels at the back, their steel-toe tips hanging a few centimetres up the wall in what seemed like a half-hearted climb, and walked back into the parlour. Mother came out from the kitchen carrying my father's food. She smiled at her husband.

But he didn't smile back, didn't reach out to slap her buttocks as he always did whether I was in the room or not. There was no sound of laughter, of shifting ceramic plates on the tray tottering on the brink of shattering because of the horseplay between two adults in love. All I heard was my mother's sharp intake of breath, the squeak-squeak of the ceiling fan, the muted tones of the newscaster on TV.

My father didn't sit up to wash his hands. He didn't eat. Instead, he looked at my mother and sighed.

'My Sweet, what is it?' she asked, taking one of his hands in hers.

'I am going to Liberia,' my father said and burst into tears.

I am the only child of my parents. The only surviving child. There were two before me and another two after me, but I am the only one who tarried, who didn't succumb to the first cough or headache that an evil wind blew my way. I grew tall and slender like my mother. But I have my father's face, the gap-toothed look that my mother said left her smitten the first time she set eyes on him.

My father named me Imoh, after himself and his father before him. He called me "Namesake" and treated me like an equal, because a medicine man had told them I was his father reborn. I even had a birthmark in my left armpit identical to my dead grandfather's.

But it was my mother who got my father's real affection. He called her "My Everything" because, as he never tired of telling me, without her he would have ended up a lorry driver like his father. It was my mother who asked him to apply to the army, who stole money from her mother, first to pay his fare to Port Harcourt for the recruitment test, and then a second trip to Lagos, for his training in Military Intelligence. When he excelled there, the army sent him to India and Russia for further instruction—making him the first man from his village to travel outside Nigeria.

Then she bore him a son to perpetuate his line.

I was almost seventeen when my father went off to war, and in all those years I never heard my parents quarrel. My father was not like the other soldiers, who came home drunk and beat their children and wives with their wide army belts. He was different from the soldiers who fought with their wives over the daily "chop money" and clothes for the children. Our home was where others came to settle their disputes, where women whose husbands were late with chop money or school fees came to borrow cash.

But that night I heard their first quarrel, and my father called my mother by her name.

'You can retire. You are fifty-six. I can help you finish the house. The supermarket is doing well,' my mother argued.

'Adia, it is not the house. I am a soldier. I can't run from war.'

'Imoh. Imoh. Imoh. Are you from Liberia? Is your father

from Liberia? Let them fight their own war,' she cried and lapsed into our dialect, which I didn't understand.

'Adia, I will not be called a coward,' my father repeated, as he had since they began. I sat stiff in the living room, the television flickering.

'You want to make me a widow. You will not make me a widow. Ah, God will not forgive you.'

'Oh, shut up, woman, and let me sleep.'

My father woke the next morning with bloodshot eyes. He and my mother did not speak, but there was no malice in their silence. It was more a gradual coming-to-terms with their fate.

I did not want my father to go to war in Liberia because things had changed in our barracks since the war began. Men I'd known for years suddenly returned in wheelchairs, with both legs gone, or with crutches digging into their armpits and one trouser leg tied up.

Meredith's father, an officer, had returned after three months with four of his fingers gone. He'd nodded off in a patrol car, and a sniper's bullet had narrowly missed his head.

After long years of peace, there was now fear. And whenever C130s landed in Ikeja and disgorged flag-draped caskets, there was grief. But before the planes touched down, the families were visited by the Harbinger.

My father left for Liberia on a Sunday. I remember clearly because I wrote my university entrance exams on a Saturday, the day before his departure. He stowed his military gear in the car and my mother sobbed as we rode with him to the airport.

'Go, don't wait,' he said to my mother, kissing her clumsily on the cheek. Tears were running down his face, and there was something like shame in his bloodshot eyes as he looked at me before striding away. 'Anyone who leaves for war without fear in his heart is the devil himself,' he'd told me days before.

For the short trip home, my mother let me take the wheel even though I had no licence. She was crying so hard she couldn't see. As I drove, I remembered the story of the soldier who, as his platoon lined up to board the plane for Liberia, had run off into the marsh around the airport.

I knew my father would never run. He would never be called a coward.

My mother did not sleep that night. When I woke the next morning, she was sitting on her side of the settee, my father's early-morning tea in place before her.

'Mummy, Papa has gone to Liberia,' I told her.

'Imoh, your namesake has made me a widow before my time.'

'Mummy, his plane has only just landed in Liberia. How can you say he has made you a widow?' I settled beside her on the settee and took the cup of tea for myself.

I passed my university entrance exams, but my father was not there to see me go off to university. I was the first person from our family to go. I wanted him there; I ached for his gruff handshake, his usual advice, 'Don't fight, son. Don't join a bad gang. Any wahala in school, come home, you hear?'

My mother, whose life now centred on her business and church, made sure I was well provided for.

But those were terrible times.

I remember nights when the Harbinger's car would drive in and wives and children would stiffen, immobilized, until it stopped in front of a house and I could hear loud wailing break out before the news was even given.

I remember also how those who had been spared the bad news would stumble indoors, relieved yet unable to feel any joy, because every new death was a reminder of how easily it could have been them.

I went to Jos, the university where Meredith had gone a year earlier. Fate had put us in the same department. I was studying law, and it was there, in one of my electives, that I learned about psychoanalysis, Sigmund Freud, and a little bit about the work the Harbinger did. He was the shrink, something new that the army brass thought would be useful.

Meredith and I became a couple in school.

We were inseparable, and on campus the distinctions that existed in the barracks— her father was an officer and mine was from the ranks—didn't matter. The university was a hammer that broke down all walls.

When we were not studying we spent nights talking about Lagos, repeating the stories rife in the barracks about who was sleeping with whom. We remembered the hapless girls who got pregnant the night they lost their virginity and the boys who stole their fathers' military firearms, went on armed robberies, and never returned.

She told me how her mother cried for an entire month after her father came back from Liberia with his fingers missing, and as we lay together in the darkness of my room, on the mattress spread out on the floor because the beds were too squeaky, I pulled her close and thought of my father and the nine months that had gone by without a single letter.

'I haven't heard from your father,' my mother would complain every time I called her on a neighbour's phone. 'He hasn't written a single letter. All I hear is "He is okay, he is okay." Why can't he write himself?'

'Mummy, Papa is fine. If anything happened to him, you-know-who would come to visit.'

'God forbid,' my mother would say.

'You know Papa is a lazy writer. It used to take him two weeks to fill out a one-page form.' This always made her laugh.

I knew my father would not die in Liberia.

My certainty wasn't rooted in anything real or easy to explain. It was just a conviction, something I believed would never happen to us, and my explanation was simple: my father loved my mother too much to make her a widow.

Meredith and I didn't go home often. Instead we stayed back in school and spent our holidays hiking in the hills that surrounded Jos. Our favourite spot was the Shere Hills, where we could swim naked and then make love on the sun-baked rocky ledges.

By keeping some distance between us and the barracks we were trying to make sense of the destruction visited on us and our friends by people from a country we knew nothing about— except that they had butchered their president and scattered his remains all over the streets of the capital city.

I finally went home when I got word that my mother had taken ill and been admitted to the military hospital. My father had been away for almost two years, without a word. We knew not to worry, because so far the Harbinger's chariot hadn't made a stop in front of our house. But my mother was tired of not knowing. The empty house, absent of husband and son, had broken her down. I was shocked when I saw how skeletal she looked.

'Mummy, what happened to you?' I sat beside her and took a bony hand in mine.

'See what you and your namesake have done to me,' she said, burying her face in the pillow.

'Mummy, I went to school,' I said, pulling her toward me.

'And your father, where did he go? To fight a war that does not concern him and to make me a widow before my time.'

'Mummy, Daddy is not dead. What did the doctor say is wrong with you?'

'Loneliness,' she said, wiping her nose with an ear of her wrapper.

That was when the Harbinger began to visit. By this time, he had started looking into the heads of the soldiers' wives too—to stop them, he said, from going crazy as more and more caskets were unloaded from C130s.

He learned about my mother's illness and came to see how he could help. He came without his car and was dressed in a T-shirt and camouflage pants– a social visit.

Opening the door, I recalled how he'd looked standing on Rita's front steps asking for a hammer. This time instead of a hammer he asked for my mother.

He had a soft voice and eyes that seemed to see deep inside you. He took my mother's hand and spoke in soothing tones.

'Your husband is okay, but I know what you are going through. Those who study war call people like you the walking wounded. Loneliness is crippling your resolve and it will cripple you too, if you let it. We must pray.'

His voice was lilting, like a pastor's, as he prayed for protection for my father, for courage in our hearts, and for strength to overcome the loneliness. We all said amen, soothed and wondering how he did it. When he visited Christians, he invoked Jesus and his father, Jehovah, and when he called on a Muslim home, he invoked Allah and intoned verses from the Quran.

Three days later, after convincing one of my mother's salesgirls to come stay with her, I went back to school.

It was Meredith who first told me about the rumour in the barracks.

'You know he sleeps with the widows,' she said as I buttoned her top. She had just had a shower and was running late for an evening lecture.

'Who told you that?' I asked as I pulled on my jeans to walk her to the gate.

'My dad told my mum and my mum told me.'

'So, the Army knows?'

'Yes, but they say they can't do anything unless a widow complains. As far as everyone can see the bastard is just doing his job. So you better tell your mum to be careful.' She got up on tiptoe to kiss me.

I pulled back. 'My mum is not a widow.'

But the thought never left me and it intensified into alarm the day the Harbinger's car stopped in front of our house.

I'd been home for just two days and was sitting inside, watching television with my mum and her salesgirl, when I heard the silence grow taut like a string being tuned. Leaving my mother, I pushed the door open.

He was dressed ceremonially, in his rank of Captain, and carried a small bag under his arm.

'It was a bomb. All that was left was his helmet and Kevlar.'

'Bulletproof jacket,' I supplied, and he nodded.

'I am sorry for your loss,' he told me, placing a hand on my shoulder.

My mother had called herself a widow from the moment my father left for Liberia, but I'd never believed he was gone for good—until that evening when the Harbinger's beat-up 504 docked in front of our house. Just as my mourning began, though, my mother's stopped.

It took her nine months—with constant badgering from my father's people, who insisted that their dead brother be given a proper burial so his wandering spirit could find rest—to accept the news and go to his hometown with me for the funeral rites.

The first Saturday after we returned was my nineteenth birthday, and I'd just seen Meredith off when a strange silence descended again. This was different, with nothing in the air to suggest grief. It was more like relief, a drawing in of the breath before a sigh.

Before I understood, I heard the neighbours screaming.

'He's back. He's back. He's back.'

I pushed open the door and there, in military fatigues, was my father. He'd lost weight and his face was furrowed with lines etched by time.

'Papa!' I screamed too and flew off the steps toward my father — my father come back from the dead, a wandering spirit lured home.

He'd showered and was dressed when my mother returned from her supermarket. She stood by the door, silhouetted against the setting sun, as if framed in a penumbra of fear and confusion.

'Imoh,' she called. And when my father answered, my mother fell at his feet and wept.

'He lied to me. He lied to me. Forgive me, my sweet, he lied to me.'

My father slept in the living room that night and the next.

There was no joy, no sense of relief. It was as if his return had caused some cosmic upheaval that left the world askew.

He didn't go out, and neither did my mother. I would wake, shower, dress, and dash off, finding refuge with Meredith, whose parents and siblings had gone to their home town on holiday.

On the third day, I was nodding off to sleep in Meredith's living room when I heard my father's voice.

'Kneel down. Kneel down. Put your hands behind your head.' The voice was calm, without a trace of anger.

I rushed out to see the Harbinger bleeding from his mouth and nose, kneeling in the street with his hands clasped behind his head.

'You killed me. You killed me and wrecked my family with your lies,' my father said. The Captain stayed quiet, bleeding and staring into the macadam.

'Stop him, Junior. Stop your father,' Meredith urged, but I made no move to stop him as people gathered.

Instead I watched. My father raised the Captain's own service pistol. I watched him place it at the back of the Captain's head. I heard the loud report and saw the Captain slump forward.

As I looked up, the people who'd gathered seemed to be smiling. There was a release, too, like a collective exhaling. I could feel it all around me: the world had found its balance once again.

Broda Sonnie

My mother said there was something they drank that made their voices sour, something that made their voices hoarse and hollow like a ghost's spectral cough.

Sonnie must have drunk it, just like the many other bus conductors hanging out of Lagos buses like demented monkeys, their raspy voices screaming: 'Oshodi o! One more yansh!'

I knew so many conductors; I met them every day on my way to and from school. I watched them scream out their routes, the veins standing out on their necks like excited snakes. They were people I saw for fleeting moments, for two or three bus stops, like figures glimpsed in a fog; men without history, without anchors. But Broda Sonnie was the only one I really knew. I knew what he looked like when he was not hanging from a speeding bus and screaming like a demon.

When I was eight years old, I told my mother that I would like to be a conductor when I grew up. The slap my mother gave me still stings today, three long years later.

'When your father left, I thought he was gone for good,' she said and flung her Scholl slippers at me where I huddled in the corner, rubbing my cheeks and crying softly. 'I didn't know he had infected you with his foolishness.'

My mother never spoke about my father except when she was angry, especially when I made her angry, and then it was always to tell me how I had been infected with his foolishness.

I don't remember my father. My Auntie Ruth told me he left when I was two.

'He ran away with a woman he used to go and drink beer with in her beer parlour. Your father, he was a serious womaniser.'

I like so many things about Auntie Ruth: the way she tosses her head when she laughs and the way her laughter thunders like a man's; the way she used to put my head between her warm thighs and cut my hair with a comb and tiger razor blade. And I liked to stand outside the window and watch her dress, knowing that she knew I was watching, yet pretending not to know.

I remember the day she surprised me as I leaned against the crack in the door.

'Oya, come inside and watch, you hear,' she said, standing naked before me, my eyes level with her dark and taut nipples. My face was flushed as I clamped a hand over my crotch to hide my rising shame. Looking down at me, Auntie Ruth laughed her manly laugh and said, 'This boy, you are your father's son.'

She was the one who spoke to me about my father: how my mother had married him against the wishes of her family; how it was love at first sight, and how my father had a roving eye and a throat that was always thirsty.

'If he didn't drink beer, he couldn't go to sleep and your mother didn't mind. You know, they say a man without a vice is a dangerous man. Your mother let him drink, but she began to worry when he refused to drink at home. Maybe it was her sixth sense, because it was when he was out that he met the woman he ran away with and broke your mother's heart.'

'Is that why mother is always so sad?' I asked.

'Yes,' Auntie Ruth said.

'But it happened so long ago,' I said and Auntie Ruth smiled
and stroked my head.

'Sometimes sadness is like a scar. It never goes away.'

My mother always told me I should not talk to Sonnie, but
I liked to talk to him. I liked to sit with him and watch him
count the dirty naira notes he came back with from work.

We called him Broda Sonnie because he was older than all
of us, but not so old as to be somebody's father. He was old
enough to work and old enough to smoke cigarettes and not
hide it when an adult appeared.

His mother was the landlord's sister and because the landlord
lived at Ikorodu and came to collect rent only once every six
months, everyone paid their money to her and called her
Mama Caretaker.

Sonnie was her only child. She gave birth to five children but
four of them had died before her husband also passed away.
So, every night when Sonnie jumped off the bus, the sound
of his slippers on the macadam echoing like a wet banger,
Mama Caretaker would hug him and then she would dance
and thank God for not letting the ever-hungry road swallow
her only son. She lived in mortal fear that the road would yawn
open one day and claim him.

Sonnie liked to smoke Simon Black and I liked to sit and
inhale the beautiful aroma, especially on Sundays when I'd sit
with him and the other older boys who came to our yard to lift
weights and shoot the breeze. I liked the way they teased one
another as they competed to see who could lift the heaviest
weights. Most of the guys came from the adjoining streets,
including Mufu, Risi's big brother and his two friends, the ones
everyone called Ayatollahs because they wore their beards long
and always dressed in flowing gowns. But after Mufu went to

Mecca, he didn't come any more and then we heard that he had bought original weights in his compound but they were only for Muslims and not for Christian infidels.

I wondered then what he meant when he called Broda Sonnie a Christian infidel because, though Broda Sonnie was not a Muslim, I never saw him go to church. Still, Mufu stopped coming to lift weights in our compound and he asked Sonnie to stop seeing his sister because he was a Christian infidel.

When someone couldn't lift a particular weight, the others would laugh and call him "woman wrapper." It was always like that and sometimes if we, the small ones, joined in the laughter, one of the wicked older boys would give the person a knock on the head if we laughed too loud, especially if the joke was on him.

But no-one beat me because they knew they would get into trouble with Broda Sonnie, so I stayed there all the time and smiled when they called me Omo Igbo– Aburo Sonnie.

I liked to watch Broda Sonnie lift weights. I liked the way the muscles rippled under his skin like caged snakes seeking escape routes. His skin was dark and rough and covered with scars that looked like malevolent tattoos, and every single scar had a story behind it.

'This one was the day we fought soldiers at Oshodi,' he would tell me when the yard had emptied and I was sitting and watching him smoke before he had his bath. 'That day, they broke my driver's head and I was just running away when the man threw his knife at me. Bastard! The knife would have entered my heart if I hadn't turned on time. Kai, you should have seen the blood. I thought I would bleed to death.'

He always spoke to me in lilting Yoruba, spiced sometimes with English words or expressions. He spoke slowly because

he said I was too Igbo to understand if he spoke as fast as
he normally did on the bus, and I always marvelled at how
normal his voice sounded at home but different once he got
on the bus, as if bus conductors had a uniform for the voice,
something they put on to disguise their real voices.

'This one *nko* what happened?' I asked, tracing a finger over
a scar that stretched from his belly button and disappeared
into his pants.

'That one, na wa!' he said, his voice dropping low to a
conspiratorial whisper. 'That was from a girl, one fine girl I
used to eye at Obalende. One day we went out and I by-forced
her. When I finished and was resting, she took a razor blade
to cut off my John Thomas. God saved me that day.'

He liked to tell me stories and he could sense that I liked
to listen and once in a while, after I had helped him write a
letter to a girl he liked, or helped him calculate his money,
he would squeeze a five naira note into a ball and stuff it into
my trouser pocket.

'Omo Igbo, don't let your mother see this money. Her wahala
is too much.'

And whenever my mother did catch me with Sonnie, she
would pinch my ear lobe between her thumb and middle
fingers and squeeze until I yelped like a dog.

'I have told you. This foolishness your father gave you must
go away, you hear?' My ear tingling, and blinded by my tears,
I would nod and say yes.

I liked to write love letters for Broda Sonnie. He'd sit on the
bed and smoke while I sat at the foot of the bed and wrote.
The things he asked me to write were things that had happened
to him while at work on the bus.

At the beginning, I wrote to many girls and most of the

things he told me to write were things he said to impress the
girls: how policemen chased him and his driver through eight
different streets; how they knocked down a policeman at an
illegal checkpoint in Mushin and refused to stop; how there
was a riot at Obalende and their bus was the only one that
escaped without a broken windscreen because no Area Boy
dared touch Sonnie Omo Edo-Bendel's bus.

But when I began to write to Risika, Sonnie stopped boasting.
He would sit on his bed, his voice low and serious as he spoke
words that seemed to come from a different person, not the
rough, hard-living conductor who defied policemen and touts.
Love made him calm, like my mother had been when she
went to the hospital to remove her appendix and they gave
her an injection that made her so slow she couldn't even lift
her hands to beat me when I spilt the Lucozade.

Risi was in the boarding house at a teachers' training institute
in Oshogbo and Broda Sonnie would ask me to write to her
every month end, as soon as her reply to his last missive arrived.

'So that by the time she has finished digesting that one,
another will be on the way,' he would say, and I would settle
by the foot of the bed, pick up my pen and paper and begin
to write, as he spoke in that strange voice that didn't seem to
belong to him.

Dear Risi,

*It's been two weeks now since I wrote to you. I am well and working
hard. I am saving money too so that I can buy that bus I have been
telling you about. It is not easy to buy a bus but if you are serious
and you can save, anything is possible.*

*For two months now I have not touched alcohol or gone to a joint
to smoke. I want you to know that I am ready to do everything you*

say if only you will continue to love me as you have promised.

I know it is only one year before you finish your TC2 and I hope that by then I will have saved enough money to buy the bus so that I can be my own oga and not have to balance anybody. Then we can get married and live in happiness.

Your brother is still fighting me but I have decided to leave him to his God Allah. They used to say my eyes are red, but if you see me now you will know that I have stopped going to the joint to smoke gbana and I know that everything will be all right.

I know you say I should not be buying you something every time I write so that I can save enough money for the bus. But don't worry, I am saving and this is just a small something for you to enjoy yourself.

It's me, your darling,
SONNIE

I liked Risi and whenever she came to see Broda Sonnie she would buy me chocolates or digestive biscuits and even though she never said it, I was sure she knew I was the one who wrote the letters. I liked the way she walked as if she was gliding on air and I used to marvel at the way Broda Sonnie behaved when she was around. He would smile the way the people who win the Lotto smile on Saturday nights on the network news.

Risi's father was an Alhaji and he had built a mosque, two streets away from ours, where all the Muslims in our area used to worship on Fridays. At first, people liked Risi's father because he had dug a borehole where people could fetch water without paying. Then he went to Mecca with Mufu and when they came back everything changed. Mufu said only Muslims could fetch water from the taps and if you were not a Muslim and you came there, the Ayatollahs would chase and whip you with koboko. Mama Ndu and the other women in my compound gossiped that a big Saudi Muslim had given Risi's father one hundred million naira to convert all the people in our area into Muslims.

'The wahala those people will cause in this area, only God knows,' Mama Ndu would say whenever Mufu drove past in his Hiace van, Islamic music blaring from the speakers he had mounted on the roof.

When Risi wrote, Broda Sonnie would call me to read out her letter to him and I remember the last letter I read out for him, the last letter that brought everything to an end. I can still remember it word for word, because after I read it to him, Broda Sonnie had dashed out of the house and I had folded the letter and stuck it into my trouser pocket.

My darling Sonnie,

I hope all is well with you?

I don't know if you have heard of Romeo and Juliet, but these days every time I think of you and me, I always think I am Juliet and you are Romeo and that something terrible will happen to us. I know you won't understand what I mean, so when I come back you must remind me to tell you the story of Romeo and Juliet.

I will finish my exams on the 16th and even though I have told Alhaji and Broda Mufu that I will return on the 18th, I will come back to Lagos on the 17th and spend the night with you. My brother has said he does not want me to visit you during my holiday and I do not want to offend him.

So prepare for me, and you will have my love all night.

I love you,

Risi

'When is the 18th?' Broda Sonnie asked.

'Tomorrow,' I said, and he screamed and rushed out of the room.

I didn't see Risi arrive. But we all knew she was in the house when we were awakened that morning by six men, led by Risi's brother and the Ayatollahs.

'Sonnie! Omo Buruku. Open this door!' Mufu screamed. As the tenants trooped out of their rooms they were met by six heavily-armed men bearing daggers, machetes and a locally-made pistol. The men asked everyone to stand aside. And we stood aside and waited until Broda Sonnie, tired of the clamour, stepped out of his room, his mother and Risi tugging at his arm and begging him to step back inside.

But he refused and there was something about him, a look of quiet acceptance and calm, that hung over him like a shroud as he walked out to the front of the compound and was encircled by Mufu and his Muslim brothers.

'Mufu, I love your sis...' he began, when Mufu stepped forward and stabbed him in the stomach.

Shock and pain colouring his face, Broda Sonnie reached for the dagger, but Mufu drew it out and stabbed him again. Then, as Sonnie sank to his knees, the other men attacked, hacking away until all that was left was a bloody mass.

Mama Caretaker's scream still echoes in my head.

Nights of the Creaking Bed

My mother was a kept woman.

It was something we knew, my brother Meze and I. It was something we knew without being told, the sort of knowledge that creeps up on you and, without announcing itself, makes your acquaintance.

We knew, and even though we didn't deny it, it wasn't something we screamed from the roof-tops. And we preferred that those who had gained this knowledge kept it to themselves.

I got my first black eye the day my classmate Damian bared the naked rump of our secret before the whole school.

'Your mother is fucking somebody's husband!'

It was enough to bring the bile to my tongue, the rage to the fore of my being, and my fist slamming into his mouth. When Damian saw a pre-molar fall out with the blood he spat out, he screamed and turned my left eye into a camera flash bulb. I saw stars.

It was all my fault: the secret that bared its rump; the premolar in the sand, the new Milky Way. I'd just seen *The Omen* and for days I'd been needling him and calling him the anti-Christ. How he'd tried to fend me off, to make me stop.

But I was like an airplane drunk on Jet A-1. I wouldn't stop. And fed up, he dredged from the pit of his rage a sentence that ensured that I never looked my mates in the eye again.

'Your mother is fucking somebody's husband!'

"Somebody's husband" was Uncle John to Meze and me. Tall, dark, pot-bellied and heavily-bearded, he cut the picture of a burglar.

He came to see my Mom twice a week. On Wednesdays and Fridays, he would arrive at about 6.30pm and park his car in the garage we had and never used, because my mother didn't have a car. Then, he would lift his bulk out of the car and walk into the house, refusing to let me carry his bulging briefcase.

I would serve him water and he would ask about school if schools were in session, or about the holiday if I was home.

'Evening Captain!' he would hail Meze. He called my brother "Captain" because he had served under a captain called Meze during the war.

'Good evening, Uncle John,' Meze would greet him.

'I remain loyal,' Uncle John would say, and then rise to join my mother in the kitchen where she would be busy preparing a delicacy for his pleasure.

With Uncle John around, my mother was a woman transformed. Flushed with excitement, she would sing old songs made new by the passion with which she sang them. Her laughter rang loud and was like music, even to ears for which it was not meant, and there was a bounce to her gait that slashed years from her age.

There was magic in those heady, fun-filled moments they spent together. And I would sit and watch and marvel at how something that brought so much joy could sire such misery and dejection in its wake, because once Uncle John left, my mother would be tetchy and grouchy.

When they had played all the LPs and danced to all the songs, they'd rise and retire to my mother's room. And once the key turned in the lock, the bed would begin to creak.

I never met my father.

By the time I was old enough to recognise faces and tell one from the other, he had disappeared to wherever vagabond husbands and vagrant fathers go, and my mother had wiped him from her mind.

She never spoke of him. She kept no pictures, no keepsakes to remember him by. Meze and I were the only reminders that there had been such a man in her life.

People who say absence makes the heart fonder never knew the kind of absence I knew. It was absolute. One that did not seem to exist, because the presence that had been, looked vaguer than the absence I lived with. I know nothing about my father. And I can't tell whether the bed used to creak when he went in with my mother.

We lived at number 56. It was large and, like all big houses, it had its fair share of gossips. We lived in front, in a two-bedroom flat. A tenement building stretched out behind us, like a tail.

Everyone saw us, Meze, my mother and me, as the rich ones. We were the ones who had a garage and could park a car if we bought one. We were the ones who never missed school because of unpaid fees and we were the ones who always had light when others didn't, because we could afford to pay our bills on time.

Our neighbours had conceived a perfect life for us, one that was free from want or lack. They knew the truth had a different face, but the overbearing misery of their own lives left them blinded to that other reality. So, to explain it away and bear up under the burden of their own lack and want, they concocted a lie which served as a palliative for what ailed them.

But it was a fragile reality. One that came crashing down the moment we stepped out of line or deigned to live as citizens of that world they said we belonged to. Their anger, like Jehovah's rage kindled at the enemies of the Jews, burned against us at long intervals because, linked closely to their awe, was an incipient fear peculiar to all poor people: that sense of dread that leaves you feeling naked because you have nothing.

One day, a neighbour unsheathed her tongue and told my mother things that made her quake. Her child had taken ill at a bad time. Doctors were on strike, which meant that government hospitals were shut. The lab diagnosed typhoid fever and the doctor at the private clinic demanded a deposit of two thousand naira.

It was evening and as she came rushing home from the hospital, it was our door she knocked on first.

'Your mama, *nko*?' she asked.

'She's not back from the shop,' I said and she sighed, a drawn-out expiration of air that seemed to drain the life out of her.

'What's wrong?' I asked, watching the tears slither down her face. 'No worry,' she said and turned.

By the time my mother came in, the neighbour's trip around the fourteen rooms in the compound had dredged up a miserly five hundred and twenty-four naira. She needed more if her child was to live.

Then my mother came back, laden with provisions and foodstuff. The woman's plea was desperate and when my mother said she had no money, her eyes turned to blazing coals rescued from a smithy.

'My son dey for hospital. If I no carry dis money go, the boy go die. Abeg, help me.'

'Mama Chisco, I have no money on me. I have just finished

shopping. I have only two hundred naira left,' my mother explained, but her words only served to fan the embers of our neighbour's desperation.

'Abeg, Mama Andrew. I take God beg you, save my pikin,' she cried.

'I can't. I have no money, true.'

A change came over Mama Chisco. She took a step backwards. She dabbed at her eyes and then she loosened her tongue.

'Okay, make I ask you one question, wetin you go do if that man wey you dey fuck, if im wife come here come catch you, eh Mama Andy? My pikin dey die and you no wan help me, eh. Why?' The woman wailed and crumpled to the floor.

My mother looked across at me. Our eyes met and I could read fear and desperation and shame in hers. Then, without a single word, she walked out of the compound.

She was gone for less than ten minutes and when she returned she gave the woman a wad of naira notes: five thousand naira in all.

The boy survived, but his mother never forgave herself. It took them six months to raise the money but my mother refused it and for years, until we left, they took to giving me money, small change, at well-chosen intervals. They hadn't become rich; they were merely making expiation for that sin.

And it was from them that I learned that sometimes the verbal pains we inflict on others can scar us for life.

My mother would have been happier if she'd been a widow. But a woman with a husband who was not there, she was more like a bat surprised by sunlight.

When you're fifteen and in the full grip of adolescence, your mother's nakedness is not the best thing to behold. So when, one evening, my mother ran out of her room stark naked and screaming at the top of her lungs, I felt a stirring that leaves me flush with shame when I recollect it.

I found her a wrapper. Then Meze and I tip-toed into her bedroom.

Uncle John lay naked and dead, his bulk filling up the bed. He was wearing nothing, save for the condom that covered his erection like a shroud.

We left number 56 soon after that and ever since I have felt, and continue to feel, like an alien in a foreign land: a radicle in search of its own clump of earth.

In the building, there were too many sniggers tugging at our sleeves as we walked past, and many eyes that suddenly began to look everywhere else but at us.

And then Uncle John's wife came to see the woman who had fucked her husband to death.

'Where's your mother?' she asked. 'She's not at home.'

'So, your mother is the ashewo who fucked my husband to death?' she asked, before I shut the door on her and the neighbours who had gathered.

Today, Meze is married and my mother is dead. When her bed stopped creaking, her heart began to slow. I am not married, but once a week I visit a widow and act as father to her only son.

He calls me Uncle Andy.

The Echo of Silence

The first thing I heard was the echo of a loud silence and then the thunder of my heartbeat as the body fell past me and landed on the floor with a loud thud.

I gasped and dropped my briefcase as a chill spread through me. I peeped down the length of the passageway. A door was being opened, so I dragged the body in and shut the door.

My heart was pounding as I turned the body over. The ashen face stared up at me and it was the face of my neighbour.

'What are you doing here?' I asked, and when I got no answer I checked for a pulse and found none. The man was dead.

My neighbour! It was absurd. We didn't even talk, except to say "hi". So why had he chosen to die outside my door?

I looked at him, at his ashen death mask and the hands that lay stiffly by his side and there was no doubt that he was as dead... well, a dead man.

But the mind is a Thomas, so I bent down to check for a pulse again. There was none. The man was dead.

I straightened up. I could have cried. I was set for work and it was almost seven. The staff bus would be at my stop in five minutes and it takes all of five minutes to get to the stop from my house. If I dallied with the corpse, I would miss the bus and I had an important presentation to make. There was no way I was going to miss that bus.

I opened the door and peeped outside. A man and a woman were conversing down the passage. I cursed and shut the door; I was stuck with the damned corpse. But I had to go, so I picked up the dead man, dragged him across the room and laid him on the couch. I locked the door, raced down the corridor, out the door and down the lane to the street corner where the bus would pick me up.

I was a minute early and sweating when the bus came to a stop. I jumped in and slumped onto a seat. I could feel the sweat inside my vest.

'Tony, is something wrong?' someone asked, but I made no reply. I wasn't in a talking mood.

'Abi, e don quarrel with im babe,' Denis joked but I shut him up with a glare.

They let me be, so I turned to the window and watched the houses and landmarks speed by. Then everything blurred, and I was back in my room with the dead man lying on my couch and pointing the way to the gallows.

And suddenly, my senses became keener as things became clearer. I was visited with the "end is nigh" vision of a man at the stake. The milling throng, the raucous chatter: everything faded as I voyaged along the wide open avenue of my mindscape.

I saw myself on my first day at school, yelling as my mother handed me to the teacher, her Judas kiss still wet on my cheeks. 'It's alright! It's alright!' the teacher kept saying but I only yelled louder. Then I saw myself after my first fight at school. My mouth was swollen but coloured with the bloody smile of victory as the teacher dragged me by the ear to the staff room repeating, as I stumbled beside her: 'We don't fight in this school. We don't fight in this school.' I remember the pain of her nails digging into the soft flesh of my ears. Then

I was before the judge. I saw him drape the black hood over his head and I screamed.

The driver stepped on the brakes and sent us all crashing forward.

'Are you okay, Tony?' he asked.

I nodded, breathing hard and avoiding the curious looks my colleagues cast me as I raised a hand to wipe off the beads of sweat on my face.

We got off the bus an hour later and I joined the others in the elevator. They were there but I didn't see them. I didn't hear them, either. All I saw and heard was the face of the dead man on my couch and the thunder of my heartbeats. 'Are you okay?' Denis whispered in my ear and I jumped.

'I'm fine, fine,' I said, as the elevator doors yawned open and I got out. My presentation was due for ten-thirty, so I sat down at my desk and tried to go over it but I couldn't. Images of the ashen face kept assailing me. I shut my eyes and tried to recall the psalm my mother taught me a long time ago: 'The Lord is my shepherd.'

But I could go no further. My memory had atrophied.

I felt a tap on my shoulder and started.

'Easy! It's just me,' Helen said, eyeing me curiously. 'The GM wants you.' It wasn't ten thirty yet, but I picked up the papers I'd prepared and walked out. Her curious and worried gaze followed me.

'Your presentation has been moved to next week. We'll have the auditor present his today,' the GM told me.

I sighed with relief. 'That's fine, sir, just fine,' I said as I let myself out. I walked back to my desk and felt relatively calm for the first time since I got into the office.

I put the papers back into my briefcase and was stifling a yawn when Helen entered with a policeman. My heart gave a lurch and I broke into a cold sweat as Helen led him to my desk.

'Tony, this is Sergeant Gideon. He's here to see you.'

I felt my heartbeat cease. My rectal muscles constricted and sweat dribbled down my armpits. I swallowed and tried to talk but no words would come.

'Hey, are you alright? You don't look too well,' Helen said, and placed a hand on my shoulder.

'I'm okay,' I managed to say. 'I have a slight headache, that's all.'

'I'll be at my desk,' she said, and walked away.

I looked up at the sergeant and in that instant I felt the image of the gallows concretise from a terrible fear. I was still caught in the vision of the end when I felt a hand on my shoulder. I jumped, as a chill ran through me.

'Sure you're alright?' the policeman asked and I could only nod my head.

'I'm here to make some enquiries about Philip Dolo,' I heard him say and for seconds I didn't know who Philip Dolo was.

He noticed my blank stare and asked: 'You know him, don't you?'

'Who?'

'Philip Dolo.' Then it hit me. Philip Dolo! 'Yeah, I know him!' I cried.

'Well, he listed you as one of his referees and I've come to make enquiries.'

'Oh, yeah!' I said, relief flooding back over me. I looked at the policeman and cracked a smile.

'What do you want to know?' I asked.

'Oh, nothing much. We'd like you to complete these forms and send them back to force headquarters.'

'Is that all?'

'That's all.'

He handed me the forms, said thanks and marched away.

The feeling of relief didn't last. I was still a wreck and I kept entering wrong figures on the spreadsheet I was working on. My mind would not stop wandering to thoughts of what lay on my couch at home and the fate that awaited me once it was discovered.

I wished the day would speed up but it crawled like a snail, leaving slimy, nervous trails all over my body. I thought I'd go mad. I wanted to leave at about three but I changed my mind and, instead, tried to fine-tune a plan. I'd get home, wait till dark and carry him up to his own door. He could stay dead forever if he wanted to. I just didn't want any part of it. At five, I picked up my briefcase and, not waiting for the staff bus, walked out of the premises and hailed a cab.

I sat back and went over my plan once again. It would work. All I needed was the cover of darkness and the dead man would be back where he belonged.

'Ah, dis kain go slow, sef!' the driver exclaimed.

I looked up to see that we were snagged in heavy traffic. 'Why you no follow express?' I asked, trying to control my annoyance.

The driver mumbled something I didn't catch, so I let him be. About thirty minutes later, we were on the move again.

Dusk had fallen and lights had come on in the houses when he let me off. I paid him and walked briskly into the building. I walked down the dark passageway, my heart pounding. I had the key in the lock when I heard my name. I whirled round, ready to run.

'Hey, what's the problem? It's me!' Dave, my friend, said.

I stared at him like I didn't know who he was. He was my friend, my best friend, but I didn't want to see him. I didn't want to see anybody.

'What's the matter, Tony? You look like you've just seen a ghost.'

'I'm...em... not feeling too well,' I stammered.

'What's wrong?' he asked with concern.

'A headache. It started at work.'

'Boy! And I came around so we could hit the town. I just got promoted.'

He was talking but I wasn't listening. I was wishing I could spirit him away from my door, make him disappear.

'You must be feeling really bad,' he said. 'Why don't we go inside and I'll see what I can do for you?'

'No!' I screamed, startling him.

'No?'

'Yes. I want you to leave.'

'Leave?'

'Yes! Leave! Now!'

'Tony,' he called, but I shut him up.

'Leave!'

Dave stared at me like I'd gone mad. Then he smiled and said, 'You'll have to shoot me first, mon ami.'

I looked at him and knew he meant it. Yet I waited for a while to see whether he'd budge. But he didn't. So, I took a deep breath, turned the knob slowly and pushed the door open. I would have to explain everything.

The room was in darkness. I shut the door behind Dave and switched on the light. My neighbour was sitting up on the couch with a bored look on his face.

'You locked me inside,' he said, as I took a frightened step

backward. 'You locked me inside.' He repeated as he rose,
opened the door and walked out.

I stood there with my mouth open, staring at Dave and
hearing in my head the echo of a loud silence.

God is Listening

My son's cries are ringing in my ears.

I put my hands over my ears, but I can still hear them. I put my head under the pillows but the voice is insistent. His cry is high pitched and blood curdling. His young, pink tongue touching his pink palate screams: 'Please, please, please.'

Last night, I finally realised what people mean when they say they have willed their hearts to turn to stone. Earlier on, I had bathed my son, creamed and powdered him, then pulled on the only new clothes he had and held him close to me, inhaling the sweet fragrance of him, letting it fill my nostrils so I would never, ever, forget what he smelled like.

Then I started walking, my son on my back, a bag containing all I owned in this world on my left shoulder. I walked and walked, weighed down with thoughts. I walked until I started wondering whether I had missed the spot, whether some supernatural and mysterious force had led me past the place I had marked and chosen for the thing I wanted to do.

But it wasn't so. The spot was there ahead of me and the moment I saw it, something like lead fell on me and began to slow me down, to nudge my spirit towards re-thinking my plan.

A passing car bathed me with light and illuminated the place I had chosen to dump my son. It was a small gate set in a wall at the back of an estate. It was the gate which drivers, nannies

and domestics of different stripes used to access the estate. I
knew that there was no way someone would not find him the
next morning.

My wish was that he would be found by the domestic staff of
a woman who was childless and looking for a child to adopt. In
fact, when my fantasies got the better of me, I would imagine
myself sitting there at the gate as they found him and being
offered the job of caring for him, just like in the story of Moses
and his sister and mother in the bible.

But I knew it would never happen that way. One: there was
no way the rich people would use that gate. They preferred
to use the big one in front where I once hung around and
sold cold water. That gate was bigger and allowed them to
drive out in their big, shiny cars (and that's why rich people
are always fat, because they are always sitting down and being
driven around). Two: Moses had a God working for him. Me,
I have no one working for me. I am not even sure God, if he
really exists, knows that I exist.

When I got to the back gate, I set my bag down, released my
son from my back and, cradling him, stuck my left nipple in
his mouth. At first, he was too sleepy to eat, but when I kept
pushing the nipple into his mouth, he started sucking.

I liked the way he sucked as if his life depended on it. It
reminded me of how Goddie used to suck on my breasts.
He would suck and suck, making sloppy sounds until I would
push him gently and tell him that my nipples were hurting.

'When you have my son, there will be war. Because we must
fight over these breasts,' Goddie liked to say as he fondled them.

My breasts were the things he liked best on my body, aside
from my hips, which he said would give him four sons. He
said my breasts were "cute and peckish" and even though I

liked the way he said it, I was always too shy to ask him what he meant.

After he had fed a while, I switched him round and put the right nipple in his mouth and while he fed, I tried not to think about Goddie because thinking about him made me happy and sad all at once.

My son fed and fed and fell asleep, and I cradled him as the tears flowed down my face. I had planned this night for almost a year, from when he was a mere foetus growing inside me. I carried him for nine months and I nurtured and grew to love him over the course of the first three months of his life, so there was no way I could dump him outside that gate, heart of stone or not, without feeling guilt, remorse and pain.

I wrapped him in the wrapper I had brought and placed him in the space between the gate and the fence. Then I lit two sticks of incense to chase away any animals that might come near him.

I bent down, kissed him on the forehead, and then turned and began to walk away. That was when he started to cry without warning. At first, his cries stayed my feet for a second, but then I stifled a sob and kept walking, my ears stopped, my heart hardened.

But the cries came on loud and clear, and the faster I walked, the louder he screamed until, scared that his cries would break my resolve and make me turn back, I started running, the tears blinding me, as I ran down the dark street like a mad woman.

'Stop or I shoot,' a male voice shouted.

I stopped. A powerful torchlight was pointed in my face and as I raised my hands to block the harsh glare, the torch was switched off and I was shrouded in complete darkness. I blinked repeatedly to get accustomed to it.

A man dressed in hunter's garb was standing before me, about two metres from where I stood. As my eyes focused fully, I noticed he was pointing a long gun at me.

'Where you dey go for this kind time?' he asked as he stepped close to me and I could smell on the breeze that blew past, the acrid smell of marijuana.

'Home,' I said.

'Wetin be home?' he asked, moving closer, his eyes searching the darkness as if expecting someone to jump out of the darkness.

'Raise your hand,' he said and switched on the powerful torch again. He beamed the light into the bushes behind me and then, satisfied that I was alone, turned to me and began to frisk me. He started from my legs, reached in between my thighs, then travelled upwards until his hands were fondling my breasts.

'Excuse me,' I said pushing his hands away but he slapped my hands back.

'Raise your hand, abi you want make I waste you?' he asked.

'No,' I said, my teeth chattering.

'Wetin dey for the bag?' he asked when he was done fondling my breasts.

'Clothes,' I said, but he didn't look inside. Instead, he turned abruptly and asked me to come with him.

We walked for what seemed like 500 metres. The night was dark and almost starless and because the man did not put on his light as he walked, I stumbled along in the dark as I tried to catch up with him.

We stopped in front of a house and I waited as he fumbled with the lock and then pushed a door open. 'Oya, come in,' he said, pushing me in. I tripped, lost my balance and fell hard against something.

It was a bed, an iron bed, and when he put on the light, I saw there was an old and dirty mattress on it.

As I knelt there crying, the man lay his gun and torch by the foot of the bed and began to undress. He took off his shirt and then the charm hanging around his neck. He kicked off his shoes, undid the string holding up his trousers and let them fall. His manhood was huge and I let out an involuntary cry at the sight.

He didn't speak to me. He just lifted me and threw me on the bed, tore off my wrapper and ripped my panties off. Then he splayed my legs and buried himself deep inside me until I was choking back tears and the sobs that threatened to overwhelm me. As he went on and on, grunting as he dug into me, I blanked out the room, his noisy grunting, the squeaking bed, the crack in the wall with the cockroach poking out its head, and all I focused on with all my mind was my son and the thought that God would keep him safe and alive until someone found him and rescued him.

When he was done, he got off me. Then, sitting beside me there, he lit a cigarette and smoked in silence.

When I woke up, it was daybreak and he was pulling my legs apart. I wanted to fight him, to scream and shout and kick, but I was too tired, so I let him. I watched him lower himself into me and then, when he had finished, I got up, picked up my bag and what was left of the tattered remnants of my pride and walked to the door. I half expected him to stop me, but he didn't.

'Where is this place?' I asked, my hand on the knob, but he just looked away and said, 'Sorry.'

That was when my tears started falling.

I sat by the door and cried until he was standing above me and saying sorry over and over again, but instead of making me stop, it made me cry all the more and, as I cried, I knew I was crying not just for the violation, but for the baby son I had abandoned and for the terrible life I now lived, the kind of life I would never ever have imagined possible. But most of all, I was finally shedding the tears I had been unable to shed that Monday morning, five years before, when I heard the terrible news that changed everything about my life.

I was two terms away from my School Certificate. We had just left the assembly ground and I was checking my maths assignment for errors before the maths teacher entered, when the principal came into the class and asked me to follow him.

As I stood up, Fidelia, my friend, waved at me to ask what I had done wrong. I shrugged and kept walking behind him. Then, as we approached his office and I saw my brothers outside, anger welled up inside me. Had they been caught smoking again?

'What is wrong with you people?' I was going to say, when the principal turned and asked us to follow him into his office and, once inside, I knew that something was terribly wrong.

My Uncle Thomas was sitting in the office, his fat stomach heaving as he snored. I had never seen him in our school and we didn't see much of him except at Christmas when he came with his kids or when, as my mother used to say, he was broke and had remembered he had a brother.

'God didn't do it well, at all,' my mother used to say to my father every time Uncle Thomas visited. 'He should have let us choose our own brothers and sisters.'

The principal coughed and Uncle Thomas roused. 'Good morning, Uncle,' we all chorused and he smiled and yawned.

'Sit down,' the principal said, clearing his throat. 'Something terrible has happened,' he began and sighed. 'I....'

'Principal,' butted in my uncle, 'These ones are no longer children. Let us tell them what has happened. See, your father and mother are dead. They died on their way back after visiting you last weekend.'

There is something that I have never really understood. Five years after my parents died and life as I knew it came to an end, I am still trying to come to terms with the questions running around my head. Where was God the day my parents died? What was God doing? Was he sleeping? Was he distracted? Was there someone praying too loudly and disturbing him from hearing the prayers my father always said before he engaged gear?

I could recite Psalm 91 from the age of five. My father taught me to say it every morning before I stepped out and at night before I lay down to sleep. It was a ritual, something my father made me teach my kid brothers. And I remember how, when I was eight, my teacher discovered that I knew the psalm by heart and told the principal. That was how I ended up in front of the school assembly reciting the whole of it to astonished senior students and classmates. The performance landed me a brand new nickname: Psalm 91.

But since my father died, I have tried unsuccessfully to recite that psalm of protection. I have never been able to go past: 'They that dwell in the secret place of the Most High...' and the reason is simple. I am not sure God is listening to me.

When we got to Lagos with my uncle, we didn't go to my father's house, the storey building we lived in at Anthony

Village. We went on, instead, to Bariga where my uncle and his family lived in a two-roomed apartment.

'Uncle, we want to stay at our house,' I told him as my youngest brother, Greg, kept prodding me to tell him that that was what we wanted to do.

My uncle looked at me as if I had just dropped from the sky. Then he belched and said, 'Listen, I don't know the kind of training your mother gave you people. But you must know one thing: your parents are dead and this is your new home. Things have changed and if I say you will stay here, then you will stay here.'

'But this house is too small,' Greg blurted out in frustration.

'God solder that your mouth!' my uncle screamed and flung the heavy ash tray at my brother. The metallic object hit him on the lips and split them. Bleeding and crying, Greg ran out of the room, with me and Sebastian on his heels.

That was how our life changed. One second, we were well-to-do kids living in a big, clean house in a quiet environment. The next moment we were living in two squalid, small, and dirty rooms and sharing what passed for a bathroom and toilet with ten other families.

Greg, who had always been the finicky baby of the family, broke out in sores in reaction to the dirt, while Sebastian fell ill with malaria. I was the one nursing and consoling and trying to calm two young boys who couldn't understand how and why their well-ordered lives had so suddenly turned into a nightmare.

After the burial in the village, my uncle called us to him. 'We are going back to Lagos tomorrow,' he said, indicating his wife and four grubby children.

'You people will stay in the village with mama,' he said, nodding to our grandmother who just smiled uncomprehendingly because she didn't speak, nor understand, English.

'We have to go back to school,' Sebastian said, jumping up. 'We can't go to school here.'

'Shut up and sit down,' my uncle said. 'We have checked and your father did not leave any money. He was spending all his money going abroad with you people and your mother. Now, he is dead there is nothing left for your education.'

'We have bank accounts that daddy opened for us,' Greg said, wiping the tears with the back of his hand. 'I know I have enough money to pay my fees.'

'You have money, eh? This burial, who do you think paid for it? Do you think money fell from the tree, eh? I see that you children are very, very ungrateful but don't worry, I know what to do. You will see my red eye. I have told you that you will stay back in the village and that is it. I was planning to pay fees for you here in the village school, but I won't pay again. You people will stay and go to farm. If you don't farm you won't eat. When I come back in two months, you will tell me whether you want to go to school or not.

Greg and Sebastian were crying but I was dry-eyed. I sat and stared at the big picture of my father behind my uncle's head.

As my uncle stood up, abruptly, to leave, my brothers rushed to him and began begging: 'Uncle we will go to farm, but please let Angie finish her SSCE. Please uncle. Please.'

My eyes welled with tears of love and gratitude for my young brothers. My uncle relented. I went back to school and, for the first time, I understood what poverty meant. I had no provisions, no new undies and no money. It was a shock for my friends. I had always bought gifts for them after spending my summer holidays in the UK, but they were the ones who

supported me now, who gave from what they had and who
encouraged me when I was not in any mood to read. All their
support paid off when I passed out of school with six As and
three credits.

From the money that my teachers and the principal gave
me, I bought a JAMB form and sat for JAMB. My score was
252 and I was admitted to study Economics at the University
of Ibadan.

Borrowing money from my brothers, who were making
money selling firewood, I took a bus to see Uncle Thomas
and announce the news.

'Uncle, I have been admitted to UI.'

'UI. What is UI? Your mates are working and getting married
and you are talking about university? If you want to stay in Lagos,
you must find a job or else you should go back to the village.'

The village was an option I did not even wish to contemplate,
so I chose the city. Since everyone agreed that I was clever, they
found me a job as an accounts supervisor in a supermarket.

The shop, almost a department store, was managed by a
woman who also ran a nursery school. As soon as I started
working there and she realised I was good with figures and
could be trusted, she put everything in my hands.

I hadn't been there long when I met Goddie. It was my
birthday and my boss had thrown a party for me, so there we
were singing and dancing when this tall, fine looking man walked
in. I was seventeen, but I knew a fine man when I saw one.

The moment he walked in, he looked straight at me and
then walked up to me, his hands folded behind him. I am
ashamed to say it now, but as his eyes bored into mine, I felt
my nipples stiffen.

'Happy birthday,' he said, as he thrust a gift-wrapped package into my hands. He had been holding it behind his back all the while.

'Thank you,' I said. 'How did you know it was my birthday?'

'I know these things.' He laughed and there was a dimple in his cheek.

After my birthday, Goddie took to coming to see me and every time he came by he would give me a gift: a pair of earrings, undies, chocolates and, later, novels when he found out that I liked to read.

I knew he was an accountant and that he had a wife and three children, whose pictures he carried in his wallet. I remember how, most nights before he dropped me off at home, we would sit in the car and talk. And now, thinking back, I realise that all that time we talked, we never ever talked about ourselves. Or rather, he never talked about himself.

I liked to listen to him. He was so full of stories and I just loved the way he talked. When he began to touch me I didn't complain because, as I have come to realise now, I was hungry for attention and he smothered me with it. Most of my friends had gone to the university and moved on. Goddie became my friend, the one I talked to, the one who listened to me. We would kiss and cuddle, but I wouldn't let him take me anywhere private. I let him touch me in the car because I knew it was safe.

'What is your ambition?' he asked me one day after I told him the story of the novel I had just finished reading. It was about a woman who wanted to be the first Managing Director of a company and battled against all odds to make it.

'I want to...' I began, but then choked as sobs rose from within. 'I wanted to be an accountant like my dad,' I managed to say.

'Why are you crying?' he asked, leaning over to take my

face in his hands.

'I am sorry. I just remembered my dad and all the plans he made for us and now they are all gone.'

'It's okay,' he said and then when I had calmed down, Goddie made me an offer, an offer that made me agree to open my legs for him.

'Marry me and I will sponsor your education.'

'Excuse me?' I said, not believing I had heard right.

'I said, marry me and I will send you to school.'

'Are you serious?' I asked, and he nodded.

'I am serious,' he said. 'Very serious.'

'Thank you,' I told him, even though I knew that it wasn't the right answer to a proposal. What I felt that night wasn't so much joy as relief.

So, I agreed to go with Goddie to a place to eat and then, for the first time, to follow him to a hotel.

'Don't worry. I will be gentle,' he said, his fingers cold against my skin.

Goddie undressed me, taking off every item of clothing as if it were made of pure gold. His kisses were feather light. He kissed me from head to toe, lingering between my legs because he said he wanted to taste me, then moving upwards and spending the most time kissing, caressing and sucking on my nipples.

He was so gentle that by the time he drew my legs apart and made me a woman, I had lost all my fears, all my anxieties and all my inhibitions. We made love twice before he took me home to my uncle's house.

It was late and there was no light on in our street when he dropped me off, and as I walked the short distance to the house under the light of the full moon, I felt as if everyone passing by could tell what I had been up to.

'Where are you coming from?' my uncle barked as I greeted him. He was sitting outside and fanning himself with an old exercise book.

'Work, Uncle.'

'Work? At 10.30 at night?' he said, his eyes blazing, and before I could elaborate on the lie, he rose and slapped me so hard I tripped and fell.

'Keep doing waka-about like your mother, you hear. When you get pregnant you will know. Useless girl.'

Goddie and I had sex every Wednesday and I always made sure that he took precautions.

'A sweet girl like you, ah, it should be skin to skin. Your blood will make me younger,' he would tell me and then sigh and reach into his pocket for a condom.

We had been lovers for about two months when, true to his words, he bought me the Polytechnic admissions forms and I applied to study Accountancy at Yaba Technical College. I took the exams and passed. When I told my uncle that I had been offered admission at Yaba Tech, he just looked at me, shook his head and said, 'You will use your yansh to pay your fees, abi?'

The admission offered me a good opportunity to leave my uncle's house. Goddie promptly got me a self-contained room at Akoka. The room served two purposes. It put a roof over my head and offered a cheaper love nest. Instead of paying N600 every time we had sex, Goddie could sleep with me as many times as he wanted and there was always food to go with it.

'You said you'd marry me,' I said to him one night as he lay beside me, my nipple in his mouth. We had just finished making love and were lying in the dark while his favourite Bob

Marley CD played softly in the background on the CD player
he bought me for my birthday.

'I promised also to send you to school, didn't I?' he said,
mumbling because he had my nipple in his mouth.

'Yes, you did.'

'And are you not in school?' he asked and I nodded. 'So,
what's the problem? You are just in ND1. If you get married
now and get pregnant, that's it. So, let's wait for you to finish
your ND at least.'

In the second semester of my ND II, Goddie insisted that
we stop using condoms.

'I have tried, haba! Which man will see young blood like
you and still use condoms? If you get pregnant I marry you,
so what's the problem? Or are you tired of me? I will leave
you and go somewhere else if you want to continue with this
condom business.'

I looked at him. If he left me, where would I go? How would
I eat, pay my rent and survive? There was no way I could make
it without him, so I agreed and this time around, Goddie came
by every night and we always had sex, whether I was tired or
not. My body was like sweet wine and he was drunk on it.

There was a riot. The college was shut down just two weeks
before our final exams were due to start. The strike was one
month old when I realised that I had not seen my period. I
told Goddie and he was so ecstatic he swept me off my feet
and danced around my small room.

'You will give me sons,' he said, dancing around me. 'Look
at your hips. These are son-bearing hips.'

'Goddie, I said I haven't seen my period. I didn't say I was pregnant,' I told him, but he laughed.

'What do you know? Tomorrow, we shall go for a test, but I already know the result: positive. I can tell a pregnant woman from a mile away.'

The test was positive. I was eight weeks pregnant and, to celebrate, Goddie took me to a Chinese restaurant on Victoria Island and then, for the first time, he spent the night in my house.

'Now that I'm pregnant, you have to see my uncle,' I told him. 'Please,' I said, nuzzling his neck.

'Okay, okay. Just give me time. Let me talk to my people who will go with me. You have to choose the right time to break this kind of news.'

I gave him time, reminding him once in a while and not really pressing it because I did not want him to get angry. Then, one Saturday in my fourth month, he came and said his people would come to see my uncle in two weeks' time. 'But we'll go and see the doctor first,' he said.

The doctor was a tall, dark man who wore very thick spectacles. He told me to lie on a bed in his office and, while Goddie looked on, he examined me. Then he rubbed this gel on my stomach and placed something cold and plastic on my tummy.

'Look at that screen. See, that's your baby. That's the heart. See how it's beating. And it's four months old,' he said pointing to two dots on the screen.

'Is it a boy or a girl?' Goddie, who'd been looking on in silence, asked.

'Hmmm.... You know, it's never exactly accurate, but let's see.' He rolled the stuff over my stomach, then looked up and said: 'I think it's a girl.'

'Wao!' Goddie laughed. 'Let me get my wallet from the car,'

he said as he rose from his seat.

I lay on that table for close to ten minutes, my top bunched up beneath my breasts. But Goddie did not come back. The doctor asked me to get up.

'You can wait outside. I have other patients waiting,' he said.

'But we haven't paid,' I said, setting my foot gently on the floor.

'It's okay,' he told me and it was the pity in his eyes that set off alarm bells in my head.

I picked up my handbag, slipped my fat feet into my slippers and turned the knob. Goddie wasn't in the waiting room. Fighting to suppress the rising panic, I pushed the entrance door open and stumbled outside. Goddie's car was not there. I sank to the ground in a dead faint.

When I woke up, the doctor, the one who had done the scan, was standing above me, a worried frown wrinkling his brow.

'Thank God,' he said. 'You gave us all a fright. Only God knows what would have happened if the mei gadi had not seen you fall.'

'I want an abortion, doctor. Please. I need an abortion.' I grabbed his arm, refusing to let go. 'Please help me. I don't want to have the child. Oh God!' I was attracting curious stares from the nurses.

'Calm down,' he said. 'Calm down. We need to stabilise you first before we can think of doing anything; moreover you are too far gone. You are already in your second trimester. And, like I told you guys, the scan is never 100 per cent sure. It could actually be a boy. We could do another scan just to make sure. Please don't do anything rash, OK?'

Two days later, the doctor said, 'Children are blessings, you know.' He had allowed me to stay on free of charge while he observed me. 'I don't recommend evacuation after three months so I won't do it, but I also want you to know that you can't tell what this child may be in the future. Women have ruled nations and will still rule nations. So, you don't know what this girl will become.'

He gave me N1000, told me to take care and bade me goodbye. It was on the bus ride home to Akoka that I realised how foolish and naïve I had been. I didn't know Goddie's home or office address. I didn't know what company he worked for. All I knew was that he was an accountant and that he was married and had three daughters.

I had never seen N1000 go so fast. Broke and pregnant, I called Goddie's GSM number and was told that it had been switched off. I sold my CD player, the one he gave me for my birthday; then I invested the money in a pure water business. The business wasn't bad, but the problem was that I was five months pregnant and it wasn't easy standing in the sun and chasing after cars with a bag of water on my head.

I quit the business after I fell and bruised my shin a second time. To stave off hunger, I began selling off my other stuff to survive. If I hadn't been pregnant, I would have sold my body. There aren't many men willing to sleep with a woman who is six months pregnant.

My landlord didn't mind, though.

'Mr. Goddie brother say Mr. Goddie don travel abroad and say you go dey pay me from now,' the man said, as he settled his bulk on my bed (since I had sold the chair).

'Yes,' I said. 'Please, do you have his brother's address?'
'Address ke? I come for my money. Which one is address?' he asked, his eyes lingering on my bare shoulders: fresh from the shower, I had been creaming my body when he announced himself.

'The agent say you no get money, not so?'

'Yes, sir,' I said, avoiding his eyes.

'Well, you get something you can give me. Lock the door.'

It went on for three months. He would come in sometimes in the morning, sometimes at night. He would tell me to lock the door. And sometimes, before he left, he would drop off a N100 note or a tin of Milo. He stopped coming after I had my son. And then, finally, the agent came and threw me out.

They say we go to hell if we die without being saved, while those who die in a state of grace go to heaven. I remember how my parents used to make us pray and read the Holy Bible out loud. I remember all that now and laugh. My parents must be wondering now what it was all about because, believe me or not, heaven and hell are on this earth.

You are in heaven if your joy outweighs your sorrow. Hell is here on earth and I have been living in it.

When I had finished crying, the hunter set out a cheap breakfast of bread and sardines for me.

'Chop,' he said and I ate.

He didn't speak to me; he just smoked quietly, casting furtive glances at me as I ate like an escaped prisoner. After I had wiped the plate clean, I emptied the sachet of pure water he gave me, belched loudly and wiped my mouth with an ear of my wrapper.

'You dey okay?' he asked, and I nodded.

We sat in silence for what seemed like eternity; then he rose, yawned loudly and said to me, 'You want to go or you want to stay here?'

I sat down there and said nothing. When I looked up at him, his face was set but his eyes were smiling.

Ahmed

For years, Ahmed had looked forward to it. Like a headstrong
fantasy that takes your sleep hostage, it had appeared ceaselessly
in his dreams.

Every time the lorry trundled into the village, Ahmed would
abandon his flock, his ears flaming with a ravenous hunger for
stories, and race to the clearing before their house. Like the
dry and thirsty earth, he would sit and lap up the stories that
dripped off his older brother's tongue.

'The roads are big, so big you can shepherd a thousand cows
and not have to walk in single file,' Yinusa would say. 'Ah, you
should see the houses, kai. Big, tall houses with a hundred
rooms and – wait!'

Yinusa would hold up a finger before accepting the bowl of
water his mother had brought him, and Ahmed would grit
his teeth to keep himself from raising his stick and bringing
it down on his brother's head. The suspense was killing him.

'You should see the houses at night. There are a thousand
lamps on the walls and you don't have to light them. Just touch
something on the wall and the lamps will come on.'

'Kai!' someone cried. The effect was the same, no matter
how many times they heard the story.

Ahmed sat there, his mind already wandering the plains,
skipping the hedges and contemplating the wide roads, the

magic lamps and charms of the city he couldn't stop thinking about.

'You have never lived until you have been to the city and kai, you should see the young women, wa yau...'

'Kai, dan iska,' his mother would say and shoo all the young men away.

While Yinusa ate, Ahmed would admire the truck he drove, the magic wagon that took you to the city. There was always that strong smell of cow urine and dung no matter how many times you washed it. The truck was transport for cattle and groundnuts and whatever else the people of the city wanted.

No one in the village drove a truck. Only two or three people owned bicycles and no more than that number had been to the city. But those had only been whistle-stops. Nobody had been to the big city, the one so far away it took days to get there and weeks to go there and return, the big city that was built on water where men who were not careful took mermaids for wives.

But Yinusa had always been a restless soul. As their mother liked to say, the village was "too small for him." Abandoning the flock in the fields one evening, Yinusa had hopped on a truck and headed for the city. No one saw him again for four long years, until the evening he trundled back into the village behind the wheels of a pickup van.

By the next time he visited, the pickup had grown into a truck and, with the growth, came more stories.

At night, before they retired into their hut, Ahmed would beg his brother to take him to the city.

'Just one time, Yinusa. Let me see those wide roads. Let me see those walls glowing with magic lamps. Let me see the sea hugging the shores. Let me touch the long hair of a mermaid.'

'You will. I will even let you suckle a mermaid's nipples if you promise to keep your mouth shut,' Yinusa would say and laugh. 'But it's not up to me. You must speak to Mother.'

Their mother had always said he was too young to make the trip, but Ahmed knew age wasn't the issue. Their mother was scared. Having lost their father and a *dan iska* son who appeared and disappeared like the wind, she was loath to let her other son follow the same trail that led to the city.

'Uwana will let me go if you persuade her. Tell her you will make sure I come back.'

Yinusa yawned and patted Ahmed on the head. 'Okay, Ahmed. Sleep now, I will speak to Mother tomorrow.'

Mother agreed this time.

Ahmed was in a fever. Excitement churned his stomach, wrecked his appetite, and kept him awake all night. And early the next morning, when Yinusa held the door to the passenger's side open for him, Ahmed shook his head and leapt into the back instead.

He loved the lulling, swaying motion as the truck roared out of the village leaving a cloud of brown dust behind. He loved watching the sun come up through the branches of the trees. He loved the gentle touch of the wind on his face. And he loved, most of all, the shimmering macadam and the mirages that loomed ahead, disappearing like hapless lakes as they approached.

He had heard the Imam speak of paradise. This must be it, Ahmed thought, inhaling the fresh air. All that was missing were the seventy-two virgins.

But the town surprised him. It was noisy, dirty and there were many people. True, the roads were paved and wider than the footpaths in the village, but he could not imagine a thousand cows trudging side by side.

'Is this all? Is this the city?' Ahmed asked Yinusa as he jumped out of the truck and stretched.

'Be quiet, Ahmed. This is just the town. Now, let's find something to eat.'

The girls who served them were all made up and scantily dressed. When one of the girls bent down to pick up the bowl of water from their table, Ahmed caught sight of her bare breasts and looked away, wondering whether she was a mermaid.

They slept in a cramped, musty room that Yinusa said was his "place". There were many shirts hanging on the wall. There were pairs of jeans and canvas shoes.

'Are they all yours?' Ahmed asked. 'Yes,' Yinusa answered, stifling a yawn. 'Can I have some?'

'Yes. But we have to sleep now, because after tonight we won't get much sleep.'

They went to the park the next day. It was noisy and dirty, too, but that was not what bothered Ahmed. What bothered him were the trucks, lots of them parked side-by-side, head to head, head to tail. Standing at the back of the truck and looking out, Ahmed felt like he had been dropped into a maze.

People passed water under the trucks and everywhere hung the thick smell of putrefaction and human waste. Ahmed wanted to ask Yinusa again if that was how the city was, but checked himself.

Everyone seemed to talk in loud voices and he had difficulty catching what was being said. He followed Yinusa, trailing far behind because he was careful to avoid stepping into the puddles of urine and stagnant water that stood all over the park.

They went into an alley where there were people standing and smoking. The smell of ganja hung thick in the air. He hated the acrid smell. The first time he became aware of ganja was the last time he saw his brother for four years, four long years during which time his father had died and he had had to grow up fast, too fast, so as to be the man of the house.

He remembered Yinusa dashing into their hut early that morning, their father hot on his heels.

'Give it to me. Hand it over,' demanded the older man.

Yinusa was chewing furiously. Their father grabbed him by the neck until he choked and spat out a globule of chewed paper and leaves.

'Keep smoking ganja and you will never amount to anything,' their father said, boxing his ears. 'The next time I catch you is the day you leave my house.'

Yinusa did not wait to be caught a second time. That evening, when he saw a passing truck, he leapt on board.

Apart from idle men smoking ganja, there were lots of women in various levels of undress, dashing in and out of doorways. Ahmed quickened his pace to catch up with his brother.

The room they entered was cramped and had that musty smell Ahmed had come to associate with the town. Yinusa shook hands with the men gathered in the room and introduced Ahmed as his mate.

'I hope he won't give us trouble,' one of the men said, speaking as if Ahmed was not even in the room.

'No. He is a good one, are you not Ahmed?' Yinusa asked but, from the look he gave him, Ahmed could tell he didn't expect an answer.

'You leave for the city tomorrow with beans and ground nuts. Isa will join you.'

'Any special consignment?' Yinusa asked with a smile.

The man did not return the smile. He sighed and said, 'You know I am still angry with you for getting us into that police wahala.'

Yinusa laughed nervously and led the way out.

The journey was long and tiring, but Isa was a jovial soul who kept Ahmed entertained. He told him the names of the towns they drove through and what to eat or drink.

'If you need a girl, I can get you one. Just tell me. You like that one with the big behind?' Isa asked, pointing, and Ahmed felt the hot flush rise to his face.

'No,' he stammered and Isa laughed.

'We were all shy the first time, but you will get used to it. And when you are ready, I will be waiting.'

They slept in Ibadan because Yinusa wanted them to get into Lagos first thing the next day. That way, they could unload early and have the rest of the day to see the sights.

'You know what they say about the big city?' Yinusa asked Ahmed, as they ate in Ibadan. 'They say, "See Lagos and die."'

'Will I die?' Ahmed asked, alarm furrowing his brows.

'No. They say that because, after you've been to Lagos, there is nothing more to see,' Isa explained.

Ahmed sat up above the sacks of beans and ground nuts and stared when Isa told him they were entering Lagos.

He showed him the sculpture of three men with arms raised in greeting. Then, as they rode into the heart of the city, Ahmed marvelled at the cars that filled wide roads, the blaring horns, the brightly-painted trucks that roared past. He stared at the tall buildings reaching almost to the skies and, over and over, Isa had to scream at him to duck to avoid ramming his head into the pedestrian bridges that stretched across the roads. He marvelled at the sight of people walking on the bridges to get across the wide roads.

'Those are pedestrian bridges. If you don't use them, the

cars will knock you down,' Isa explained.

They rode deeper into the city and Ahmed could not stop staring. This was more than he had expected: the sheer number of people, the wide roads and vehicles of all shapes and sizes.

'We are now in Iganmu. We will park and then go get something to eat,' Isa explained.

Yinusa was looking for a good spot to park and Ahmed watched as Isa picked up a piece of wood that had been lying atop the bags since the beginning of the trip and began to poke at iron cables that dangled low and close to the truck.

'Sit down and be careful,' Isa told him.

As Yinusa manoeuvred the truck into place, Ahmed spotted one of the cables dangling close to the truck and, rising to his feet, reached out to push the cable away.

There was a tingle on his fingertips. Then he felt as if someone had punched him in the small of the back. He heard Isa scream his name, but when he opened his mouth to scream back, smoke escaped instead and then he was jerking and flying through the air.

By the time Yinusa and Isa got to him, Ahmed was dead and lying face down in the torpid water.

Buzz

It was a wet morning and Buzuzu was standing outside a blue, run-down building with a frown on his face. Those who knew him would not have thought anything amiss because Buzz, as friends preferred to call him, was forever frowning, as if he held a perpetual grudge against the world.

He had on a black leather jacket. A black fedora hooded his eternally-bloodshot eyes while a well-pinched and half-smoked cigarette burned slowly between his fat, dark lips, the smoke curling up into his face. A policeman watching him from a distance wondered whether it was the smoke that made him squint.

Buzz was in a foul mood, but this was nothing new because Buzz was always in a foul mood. Today was different, though: the dead, big-bosomed woman lying in the puddle at his feet was someone he used to know.

Buzz looked at the dead woman and then flung the half-smoked cigarette into the overflowing gutter. He circled the woman, looking for something only the experienced eye could see. Buzz was a homicide detective attached to the Pedro police station. A twelve-year veteran, he was the go-to man whenever a stiff turned up.

Behind him, a woman's voice was raised in fevered explanation, as if she had been accused of the murder.

'I open door this morning make I piss and the deadi body just tanda for there.'

Ignoring the raised voice that answered a question no one had asked, Buzz regarded the body with a cocked eyebrow. Bending down, he looked past the woman's wide open legs, glossed over her pink panties and focused for some time on her enormous breasts. There was something glinting deep between them. Buzz reached in and fished out a necklace and pendant. It was a gold pendant, inlaid with four stones. It looked expensive and out of place on the shabby corpse. He turned it around, and on the other side was the inscription: *"To Nana with luv, Otunba."*

Buzz straightened, lit up and began to walk away with brisk, long strides.

'Buzz, wetin you want us to do?' a cop asked and, without breaking his stride, Buzz flung a crisp reply over his shoulders.

'Do your job, Mister Man.'

Nana had worked as a waitress and dancer at No. 7, a seedy bar tucked into one of the labyrinthine streets in Shomolu.

Buzz had once been a regular for what, seven, eight months? Always on the move, he never dallied anywhere for too long because quotidian routine always left him bored. Which was why he loved his job. No two murders were the same. Every murder, whether pre-meditated or not, had its own signature, its own peculiar DNA, and it was up to people like Buzz to look beyond the surface to see what others could not see.

It was at No. 7 that Buzz first crossed paths with Nana.

'You have a spare cigarette?' she asked, sidling up to the high stool beside Buzz.

He didn't say a word; he just shook out a cigarette and held it towards her. She took it and stuck it between her lips but made no move to light it. Sighing, Buzz produced his lighter and lit her cigarette, then turned to his beer. He had watched her dance night after night and, though he liked how she moved her fluid and full-figured body on stage, he didn't want her sitting next to him and making small talk.

'You come here all the time and you never talk. Did somebody steal your tongue?'

'No, no one stole my tongue,' Buzz said, surprising himself by even bothering to answer. 'I just like to look.'

'Is your name Lookman?' she joked and laughed and, surprising himself again, Buzz laughed too.

'Are you married?' she asked, letting out a perfect ring of smoke.

'Nope,' Buzz answered.

'But you have a girlfriend?'

'No.'

She looked at Buzz, and then burst out laughing.

'Buy me a drink and I will be your girlfriend for tonight,' she told him, tapping her long fingers on the formica top of the bar.

'I don't need a girlfriend for tonight,' Buzz said and looked at her from beneath his black fedora.

'Buy me a drink and I will leave you alone,' she said and laughed her girlish laugh again.

Buzz bought her a drink, but she didn't leave him alone. She told him her name was Nana and that she was born in Ghana. She told him she was pursuing a part-time degree programme at the state university and was dancing in bars until something better came along.

Buzz didn't believe her but he played along, because he

was suddenly keen on seeing what her big breasts looked like when they were set free. And, it had been a while since he'd last had a woman.

He found out what her breasts looked like four hours and six bottles of beer later, when they both stumbled, half-drunk, into his two-bedroom flat. They kissed slowly as they fell into bed. Then he divested her, taking her top off and gasping when he undid the clasp of her bra and two watermelons sprang at him.

They made love twice before he fell into a deep, dreamless sleep.

Nana was gone by the time he woke up. He checked for his wallet and the gun he kept under his pillow and, satisfied everything was alright, went back to sleep.

Buzz went straight to the police station and wrote his preliminary report. Then he made some calls to a few people he knew, people who made it their business to know the kind of things people like Buzz wanted to know. When he was done, he lit another cigarette, put his legs up and shut his eyes, his mind wandering.

Buzuzu's ambition had been to get into the military and become an officer. He was intelligent, had left school with good grades and believed he could make it to the Military Academy. He bought the forms for the entrance exam. He passed the exams but was not admitted. He made three more futile attempts before he finally had to accept that getting into the elite academy depended on more than intelligence.

'Let us go to Lagos,' his father had said. 'We will go and see my cousin. He retired from the army five years ago. I am sure he can help.'

But when they arrived, the cousin's house was in turmoil.

Children were crying and women were bawling, while the men
stood around with arms folded across their chests, pretending to
be strong. That morning the former soldier had been attacked
and stabbed to death while out running. One of the blows had
been so bad, it severed his jugular.

Buzz felt not so much grief as a sense of deprivation. It was
as if, by dying, his father's cousin had joined hands with all
his other real and imagined adversaries to deprive him of his
dream.

It was that night, after most of the mourners had gone and he
was lying wide awake on the mat beside his sleeping father, that
he had had his road to Damascus experience. In a moment of
clarity, the face of the dead man's widow had loomed before
him in all its grief-stricken ugliness and Buzz vowed, there
and then, to make sure that no murderer ever went scot-free,
if he could help it.

'Papa, I want to join the police,' he told his father the next day.

Homicide was a natural choice. His success rate was high
because he was thorough and detailed in his investigations, with
a natural nose, colleagues and superiors agreed, for sniffing out
murderers. But sometimes, there were obstacles where men
of power and influence suddenly appeared on the horizon,
obscuring the landscape of an investigation with their shifty
eyes and their blood-stained fingers.

'Take it easy, Buzz,' his Divisional Police Officer told him
once, when an investigation led them to the doorstep of a rich
and influential politician. Rising from his seat and coming to
perch by the edge of the table in front of Buzz, he placed an
avuncular hand on the young man's shoulder and said, 'Our
job is to serve and protect, but remember we are only too
human and, most of all, remember it's just a job. So take a

week off, go and see your parents in the village. By the time you come back, we will have sorted this out. Someone else will die and you will do what you do best. But on this one, your job is done.'

Buzz rose, saluted and walked out, a lump in his throat.

His DPO was right. There would always be two sets of rules, one for the rich and one for the poor, but the DPO was wrong about one thing: his work as a homicide detective was not just a job. It was a calling.

No. 7 looked different. The walls had a new coat of paint. The long stools were new and the formica top had given way to tiles. Buzz ordered a beer. He drank, belched and lit a cigarette.

'Excuse me,' he said, motioning to the bartender. 'I am looking for Nana. Has she come in today?'

The barman shook his head. 'I never see her. You know say she no dey work here again.'

'Oh, I never come here in a long time. Where I go see Nana?'

'I no know. But she come here yester-night with Mr. Next-door.'

'Ok. Next-door don come in today?'

'No, but if you wait small, you go see am when e come in.'

'Ok. Give me another beer and one for you,' Buzz told him and sat down to wait.

Buzz waited till past midnight, drank two more bottles of beer, bought the barman, who said his name was Jango, as many bottles, then stood up to leave when Next-door still hadn't shown up at 2am.

'If e no come today, e go come tomorrow,' Jango said, slurring his speech and holding out Buzz's change. Buzz waved him off, said goodnight and went home.

He was back the next night and the one after, but Next-door didn't show up. It didn't stop Buzz from enjoying his drink, though, and, watching the girls dancing on stage, he remembered the night Nana had come to him at the bar and asked him whether his name was Lookman.

On the fourth night, Next-door ambled in. Buzz thought he looked like shit. Tall, dark and lean, he wore his guilt like a tattoo. It was so bad, you could see it even if you weren't looking. The moment he stepped in, Buzz knew he was the man, even before the barman nodded to indicate that his quarry had arrived.

Next-door had one drink and then rose to leave. It was obvious that he had come expecting to meet someone or have someone join him because he kept glancing at the door and looking at his wrist watch. Buzz gave him a minute's lead before he drained his glass, slapped a five hundred naira note on the bar and headed out after him.

Next-door was standing beside a car and passing water when Buzz came out of the bar and began to walk towards him. Something, a sixth sense or primordial warning system, must have set off an alarm, because the moment Next-door looked up and saw Buzz crossing the street, he cursed and began to run, trailing urine as he sped down the street.

Buzz gave chase but Next-door was fast and fit and as Buzz increased his pace to catch up, he cursed all the cigarettes he had smoked, all the pinched butt-ends crowding the old glass bowl that served as an ashtray in his room.

Next-door tore down the street, turned the corner and leapt over a parked car. Buzz burst out just in time to see him crash into a couple and the three of them fell in a heap. Buzz increased his pace, his heart pounding as he laboured to narrow the lead. But Next-door was up in a flash and running with a slight limp. He turned another corner and burst out on Bawala Street. Next-door jumped over the gutter and stopped suddenly. In a brief moment his body was illuminated by the headlights of an oncoming vehicle.

Buzz saw the car hit Next-door, who flew up and rolled over the roof to land on the road with a loud thud.

By the time Buzz reached him, a small crowd had gathered.

'Police! Police!' Buzz said, panting and clearing a path through the crowd. He felt for a pulse on the bloody and bent neck, but found none. The man was dead. Buzz searched through Next-door's pockets with one hand, keeping the other on his gun, his senses alert to the eyes in the crowd watching him. He pulled out a wallet and rifled through it. Inside were naira notes and call cards. On the back of one of the cards was a phone number and address, hand-written in blue ink. Underneath, in a different scrawl, someone had added Otunba Bakare in red ink, followed by a phone number and note in blue that said, "meet Otunba at No 7 by 8pm." Buzz was sure Otunba Bakare was the same Otunba who gave Nana the necklace, but he was not so sure that the number in blue ink belonged to the name in red.

Buzz pushed the wallet back into Next-door's pocket, palmed the card and reached for his mobile. He dialled a number and spoke rapidly into it. Then he put it back in his pocket and began to walk away.

'Hey, who go carry dis dead body?' someone screamed, but Buzz just kept walking.

Back at home, he set the card down on his table and gazed intently at it, as if by staring hard at the blue and red scrawl, the answer he sought would jump up and smack his forehead with a thump.

Who was Otunba and why was he turning up like a bad penny everywhere he looked? Why did Next-door run when he hadn't even been asked a question? What was Otunba's name doing on a card in Next-door's back pocket and on the pendant of a dead woman? Still ruminating on these and other questions, Buzz shrugged off his sweat-drenched clothes, stepped into the shower and cursed when the water didn't come spurting out. He scooped water into a bucket from the reservoir he kept and showered with that, while his mind wandered.

He slept fitfully, rising early to go to the police station. As he entered, he saw a young, prematurely-aged girl lying on the bench behind the counter. She had on heavy make-up and her lipstick was smudged. Her short skirt had ridden up to expose blue panties. Buzz stopped and tapped her on the shoulder.

'How is your father?' he asked when her eyes fluttered open.

'Wetin? Abeg leave me alone,' she snapped, and went back to sleep.

She was a prostitute, but Buzz had known her years earlier when he was a rookie cop and she was a prepubescent teenager with a penchant for tight clothes. Her father was his landlord then: a hard-drinking, skirt-chasing husband of four wives and father of fourteen children.

Acknowledging greetings from his colleagues, Buzz went to his desk and opened the drawer. He updated his report, adding details of the chase and the fatal crash that claimed Next-door, but leaving out every reference to Otunba. No need to get thrown off the case. Then, he checked his gun, holstered it and, picking up the card, set out for Oyadiran estate in Yaba, the address on the card.

Buzz asked the okada man, the driver of one of the ubiquitous second-hand bikes that serve as quick transportation for many Lagosians, to let him off four houses away from No. 387. Then he walked all the way down the street before sitting at a mallam's shed and ordering cigarettes, even though he had a pack in his jacket. Pulling his fedora down over his eyes, he smoked slowly while his gaze focused on a house with a small black gate. It was an insignificant house, made more prominent by the very reason of its insignificance. It looked out of place in the midst of the stately, well-appointed houses that lined the quiet street, occupied mostly by expatriates and Indian merchants.

It was the kind of house that seemed to scream out a silent warning, the kind of place where people entered and never came out again. The gate was set into a corner of the wall and someone had defaced it with a deranged scrawl that started with an F and ended with what looked like a k.

Buzz sat and waited for the length of time it took for him to smoke six cigarettes and watch two men, one short and bushy-haired, the other tall and gangly, park an old Mercedes Benz outside and disappear through the gate.

Buzz waited until they came out again. Then he dialled the number on the call card, and to his surprise, the short man answered on the second ring. Buzz ended the call and dialled again just to make sure.

This time he let it ring and then heard the gruff voice say, 'Haba, who is this?' the question carrying across the road to him.

Buzz ended the call again and began walking, his eyes scanning the road for an okada, as he heard the old Benz cough to life and begin to move. The Benz was already about one hundred metres away when he found a bike.

'Quick. Follow that Mercedes.'

Buzz was just in time to see the Benz turn off at Atan cemetery and head towards Customs.

'Just go slow, no run too much,' Buzz told the okada man as he handed him a two hundred naira note. The Benz burst out at Abule-Oja, drove all the way to the Unilag gate and turned left towards Akoka. At Pako, the driver turned left and then made a series of turns until they were at Fola Agoro.

When the Benz came to a stop, the short man got out and went to a tyre shop. He spoke to a beefy man who was naked from the waist up. Buzz paid the okada man and watched as they spoke. Then, when the short man returned to the car and the car started moving, Buzz hailed another bike and gave chase.

As the car meandered through the crowded streets of Shomolu with its many printers' shops, Buzz had an overwhelming feeling that he knew where the Benz was heading and he gave himself a mental pat on the back when it came to a halt in front of No. 7.

As Buzz watched the men go into the bar, he knew at once that this was where the story was meant to end because this was where it had all begun. He paid the okada man and reached into his jacket to check his holstered gun. Satisfied, Buzz crossed the road and approached the bar.

The gate was open. Buzz checked to see that there was no one at the door. Then he entered the compound, pushed the door open slowly with his right foot and edged into the dimly-lit space.

He made out three men as his eyes adjusted to the barely-lit interior. There was the barman looking cowed as he stood in front of the two men. The tall, thin one was seated, a cigarette burning between his lips, while the short one had a gun in his hand.

'Otunba, make I waste this guy? He is lying to us,' the short man said, waving the gun around like someone high on very cheap drugs.

'Tell us the man name and we go leave you alone,' the Otunba said in a wheezy voice.

'I no sabi the man name. E come here and e ask for Mr. Next-door. The first night, e no see Mr. Next-door, then the day wey e see Mr. Next-door na im we hear say car don kill Mr. Next-door.'

'The man come here two days and you no sabi im name?' the Otunba asked and the barman nodded.

'E no ask my name and I no ask im name,' the barman lied.

'Otunba, dis man dey talk nonsense,' the short man said and hit the barman on the head with the butt of his pistol.

'Don, easy,' the Otunba said as the barman screamed and raised a palm to check whether he was bleeding.

'Tell us the man name and we go leave you alone,' the Otunba said and stood up.

'Put your hands up!' Buzz barked, gun in hand as he strode towards them.

The short man was fast. Buzz didn't even see it coming.

One second, he was raising the gun, its nozzle pointing downwards. The next second, the gun was spitting fire. Buzz crouched low as the bullet whizzed past, and then he let off two shots and saw the short man drop. By the time he rose to his feet, the Otunba had dashed behind the bar and disappeared.

'Stay here,' Buzz said to the barman, as he picked up the dead man's gun and gave chase. A door led outside. Buzz kicked it open, waited a heartbeat, and then poked out his gun hand slowly.

He felt the swoosh of air a split second before he felt the

searing pain shoot up his right hand as a metal pipe connected with his hand and knocked away the gun. Cursing and grunting in pain, Buzz bent low to evade a second blow aimed for his head and then he was standing and staring at the Otunba, who was now wielding the weapon and trying to push Buzz as far away as possible from the gun that was lying on the ground between them.

'Otunba, put the pipe down,' Buzz said.

'God punish your mama,' the Otunba hissed and thrust the pipe at Buzz. It connected with his ribs and as the pain spread, Buzz reached into his left pocket and retrieved the short man's gun. He raised it and saw the surprise on Otunba's face.

Buzz smiled and squeezed the trigger.

Onions

I didn't have new clothes.

My mother said she forgot. I remember that. I also remember that it was Christmas, and nothing much besides. Ah, but I remember that I was sad, so sad that the bile rose to my tongue and made my eyes dim. I was sadder than I had ever been and I had been sad a whole lot. I was so sad, I could reach out and grab a handful from the sadness that hung low like a dark cloud over my head.

I was a kid then, but old enough to know that I was the only one in the whole world who didn't have new clothes. I also knew that our neighbours had prepared feasts while my mother had prepared nothing.

And of course it made me sad and angry, like the run-away preacher in the bible who slept under a tree and woke to find it had withered.

It was Christmas and everyone was at a feast from which fate and circumstance had banished me. It was a cold morning and instead of getting up, I lay huddled up on the thin mat that had long ceased to protect me from the cold of the floor.

When I rolled over, my mother kicked me on the shin. I jerked my leg away and opened one eye to spy on the world. The world I saw was a small, cluttered room with a thin sliver of light cutting it in two.

My mother was awake and scuttling about like an excited rat. She rattled tins and pots, swiped at mosquitoes and cursed each time she missed. I opened the other eye and the world exploded. The world is a small place for the one-eyed. 'Good morning, ma!' I tossed at her as I rose and headed for the door to piss.

'Who are you leaving the mat for?' My mother's voice came at me like a hungry policeman with a baton. I stopped, turned and folded the relics of what had once been a mat. I stuck it under the bed and walked to the toilet.

My mother was in a foul mood so after I pissed, I dallied outside, like a ghost surprised by sunlight, to watch the other children being scrubbed for church.

'Dele, I'll show you my Christmas clothes!' Seni yelled at me as he tried to get the soap out of his eyes.

'Okay,' I threw back, and fled.

I didn't have new clothes and it was Christmas.

I sneaked back inside, like a thief, but my mother saw me. Our room was so small, you had to be invisible not to be seen. Sometimes I felt like we were sticks of cigarettes and the room was our pack. And when my mother got into a foul mood, it contracted to the size of a matchbox.

'Oya, go and wash your stinking mouth,' she flung at me as I leaned on the wall and watched her exertions. The day was yet a virgin but my mother was sweating like a woman in labour.

I picked up my brush, filled up a cup, put a dash of salt in my palm and went outside. Outside the sun's shy smile had grown bolder, so I sought the shade of the eaves. I brushed my teeth and cleaned my tongue, feeling my mouth awaken to the sting of salt.

As I gargled, Seni appeared in jeans and a T-shirt. He wore

his old tennis shoes. 'I don't like my new shoes,' he announced as he caught my gaze. I didn't know what to say, so I went on gargling.

'Are you coming to church?' he asked. I shook my head and gargled some more. He said something else, but I missed it because of static in my ears and then, just as suddenly as a crazy rain, my eyes began to spit tears of pain and shame.

I spat out the water and ran inside, leaving my friend to wonder. He didn't like his new shoes. I didn't even have new shoes.

My mother let me be, which was a good thing. I sat on her three-legged bed and watched her. She emptied cans, counted the small bundles of salt she had set aside the previous night, checked how many onion bulbs she still had, and stood facing me. But she didn't see me. She wasn't even looking at me.

I knew the look: the long, melancholic stare that shot through the tattered boundaries of our lives to traverse the craggy terrains of a sad past that sired a present that was even worse.

We didn't have a future. It was too much to hope for. We lived for the moment. The next minute was like an age and we had to journey to it on the ship of willpower. Despair had gnawed away at our hope and turned it to dust.

I sat there and watched her until the dull light left her eyes and she let off the long hiss that signalled the end of her contemplations.

My mother turned suddenly and grabbed my hawking tray. Panic seized me. She started counting and throwing the onion bulbs onto the tray and I opened my mouth to speak, but no words would come. Tears stung my eyes like the salt that woke up my mouth every morning.

There were twelve bulbs in all. She pushed the tray towards me and said: 'Get up and go. We need the money.'

That was when disgust laid healing hands on me and unstopped my tongue.

'No, Mama!' I screamed, the tears falling down my face.

'Take it, and go. We need the money!' she yelled, boxing my left ear. She knocked me against the door and kicked the tray to me. I picked it up and fled outside.

When I turned to look, she was standing at the door and yelling, the veins on her neck standing out like cobras poised to strike.

'If your father didn't drink himself to death, we wouldn't be like this!'

I walked out, the tray on my head, through the sea of children who had dammed themselves on both sides to allow me to pass. I walked past them, blinded by tears and anger, into the sun.

I walked past the thronging spectators at the festive arena, past children hurrying to church in their new clothes and past men already drunk and staggering.

There was a feast of joy all around and I was the lone mourner. I had a tray full of onions, a shirt full of holes, a voice that refused to call out my wares and eyes that rained tears.

I stamped through the streets, watching gaily-dressed children glide past, and I died in instalments. There was no joy, no sadness. Only emptiness. I made no noise. No one would buy my wares. No one bought onions on Christmas day. I walked on, until I came to a big house with a big fence and a big mango tree.

I sat down in its shade, put my tray beside me and scanned the street. It was quiet. A dog barked once or twice and the wind bore vagabond strains of a sad song to my ears.

I sat there and thought of the father I didn't know, the one who drank himself to death. I didn't know how somebody could drink himself to death. Though once, because I was hungry and there was no food to eat, I kept on drinking water until my stomach bulged and my eyes dizzied, but I didn't die.

My mother drank a lot, too. Not water. She drank a lot of gin. It made her thin and she looked like a witch. Then one night she woke me up with her screams.

'Call the landlord! Call the landlord! I've got crabs in my stomach!'

I fetched the landlord and our neighbours and they ferried her to the hospital. I thought my mother had gone mad. But they said she had an ulcer and asked her to quit drinking or die.

She said she didn't want to die and she didn't want to stop drinking, either. They asked her to choose. I think she made the wrong choice because she is dead now.

I heard footsteps and I looked up. A man was going past. I knew him. He used to come and see my mother when I was younger. He was one of those who slapped my mother's buttocks, and my face if I stared. He slept over a couple of times but I didn't like him because he snored too loud.

I waved and said, 'Good morning!' But he just walked on. He didn't remember me, but I remembered him. 'Grown-ups don't remember much,' I told my mother once and she said it's because they have too many things to think about. When I asked what things, she laughed and said, 'Like children who ask too many questions.'

That's one of the rare occasions I recall seeing my mother laugh. I liked the way she laughed, soft like the tinkling of bells, and she had a nice smile that was as bright as a big chunk of the sun.

But the pain, the despair, and the drink made her forget how to smile.

The shade was soothing and I soon fell asleep. I slept for a long time because the sun was way up above my head when I awoke. I gazed about in sleepy-headed confusion. Something had forced me awake. A sound! I looked down the road and saw him. He was rolling along on his wooden trolley and pushing himself with his muscular arms.

I watched him approach, the cranky noise of his trolley waking up the somnolent afternoon.

He was squat, all trunk and no limbs. And he was gaily dressed, in the mood for Christmas. He had a huge smile plastered on his face as he trundled past me: a cripple dressed for Christmas and trundling along on a trolley he propelled with his dusty hands.

I watched him fade to a speck in the distance and gleaned the ripe ears of a simple truth.

Hunger gnawed at my insides and I remembered the meal Seni's mother had promised me the day before. I picked up my tray and dusted my shorts. I knew where I had to go. Home! It was Christmas and I was tired of being a stranger at life's feast.

I began the walk home. I knew my mother would beat the hell out of me. I knew I would cry like hell. But I didn't care.

It was Christmas.

The Devil's Overtime

My mother wanted to see the world, but I was like a noose around her neck, a piece of rope that tethered her to the village, a swollen foot that would not let her run with the wind and take flight.

She used to sit outside my grandparents' house, chin in palm, while her eyes stared into the distance wondering what could have been. I'd sit and watch, even though I pretended to be playing with stones. Sometimes, when I thought she had fallen asleep, her long drawn-out sighs would remind me that she was not asleep, just lost inside her own head.

She was happiest and saddest when an old friend, who had left the village, returned with tales of the city and how wonderful things were there. My mother would be full of questions, the way a boil is full of pus, and when the friend left, my mother would lie on her bed and cry.

My mother didn't speak much to me. She made sure I was clean and fed and out of the way. I didn't mind, until my grandparents both died two months apart. That was when I began to notice that my mother really didn't want me around.

My father lived two villages away. My mother said he was my father, even though he never, ever, spoke to me, nor called me a son.

'See, see your useless father,' my mother would say when

she took me with her to the market to cut my hair.

But my father would laugh and say, 'When will this your madness end?'

Whenever he said this, my mother would curse him and push me hard, urging me to move fast as if I was the one who made him refuse to acknowledge that I was his son, and while we stumbled along, the man she called my father would blow cigarette smoke into the air and laugh.

Everyone said he was my father because, according to them, we looked alike. He was dark like me and he had bow legs like mine. He also had ears like mine, the wide, open ears that made my classmates call me "Batman". I guess my mother had hopes that, one day, my father would finally take a good look at me and acknowledge that I was his son after all.

I was nine years old when my mother said we were going to Lagos.

'If you don't run, can you count the miles?' she asked me as she buttoned my shirt, and I shook my head. 'You see? One day I will wake up and I will be sixty years old and I will ask myself, "What have you done with my life?" Will I say, "I had a baby boy whom his father rejected"? Is that what you want me to say?'

'No,' I said, and she sighed.

'It's not easy for me. If I was alone...' she said, and left it hanging.

I was getting used to it all now: her constant 'If I was alone, life wouldn't be like this.'

When my grandmother was alive, my mother didn't bother me too much with what would have been if I hadn't been born, because every time she did, my grandmother would hiss and say to her, 'Did anybody force you to spread your legs for that good-for-nothing?'

I didn't want to go to Lagos but I also wanted to, because the fact that I was going there had brought me new-found respect. My friends looked at me like I was going to the moon.

'You will see big bridges and houses taller than trees,' someone said.

'And the roads; they say you can't cross them because there are like a hundred cars passing at the same time,' said another.

'You will tell us about it when you come for Christmas, abi?' another asked.

I nodded and looked away. I had lied to them that we would be staying with my uncle, even though I had no idea where we were going to live. And I didn't know whether we would be coming back for Christmas.

It was my father who came to pick us up on the day we left for Lagos. My mother and I sat in front, while the market women sat at the back with basins stacked high with their purchases. We looked like a family taking a leisurely ride. That is, if you took a picture of us in front and cut off the women at the back.

My father smoked with his left hand, while his right hand gripped the steering wheel. My mother sat me in the middle and, all through the ride, stared fixedly out of the window.

My father did, at least, acknowledge my presence on the short ride to Asaba, where we were to board a bus for Lagos. When he finished smoking his second cigarette, he flicked it into the bushes and pulled out two tablets of tom-tom from his breast pocket. He popped one in his mouth and offered me the second. I was reaching out to accept it when my mother slapped it away. My eyes clouded with tears as I stared downwards, focusing on a hole in the floor of the car, through which I could see the road.

'This madness of yours, when will it stop?' my father asked her, before lighting another cigarette.

The luxury bus smelled like new shoes. My mother and I sat in the middle. I had the window seat, from where I could watch the hawkers selling everything from biscuits to gin, wrapped up in sachets. There were very many people hurrying and trying to catch their buses.

A fat woman, who'd arrived late, ran after her bus, which was already leaving the park.

'I have paid. I have paid,' she cried, waving her ticket above her head with her free hand while the other hand dragged a travel bag along. The bus squealed to a halt; the conductor jumped down and, cursing her, pulled open the boot at the back. As he took the woman's bag, it snapped open and spilled its contents. Falling on her hands and knees, the fat woman began to pick up her stuff, a bra here, a blouse there. Behind her, the conductor picked up the biggest pair of panties I have ever seen and was waving them above his head as people laughed.

'What's funny?' my mother asked, giving me the look, the one she gave me before she slapped me and made me see stars. This time she didn't slap me. She just looked at me, said something about my father, and hissed.

'I want water,' I said a few minutes later as our bus made its way out of the park, but my mother just glared.

'You want to piss inside the bus, abi?' she asked, but I was smart enough to say nothing.

I looked out of the window as the bus hurtled on its way to Lagos, eating up the distance like a carnivorous monster. My mother did not look at, nor speak to me. She stared straight ahead, her eyes unblinking. I ignored her, too, wishing my grandparents were still alive so I wouldn't have to make this trip.

'Take,' my mother said and gave me a sausage roll and a can of Coke. I said 'Thank you' and ate, chewing on the stringy sausage roll and sipping the tepid drink.

As I ate, I did not tell her that what I really wanted to do was whip out my *pingolo* and piss, for fear that she would hiss and slap me. Instead, I held it in, sweating and moaning softly while my bladder threatened to burst.

Finally, we made a stop at a place called Ore and everyone got down so they could piss and stretch their legs. 'Forty minutes! Forty minutes, o, or we go leave you for this place!' the conductor screamed, a vein standing out on his neck.

I ran to a bush and pissed for almost twenty minutes, or so I thought, because the stream of urine seemed to go on forever in a warm fountain. I slept for the rest of the journey and only opened my eyes when my mother hit me and told me we were in Lagos.

Lagos was madness. Watching the crowds, the innumerable people stuck in what I supposed was perpetual motion, almost made me dizzy. Looking at the people in Lagos was like looking into a gigantic whirlwind, but instead of bits of rubbish, what we had inside was an eddy of human beings.

We got down from the bus at Ojota and, grabbing my hand while the other one held onto the new travel bag she'd bought the previous week, my mother led me a short distance to where we boarded another bus, a small yellow one. I sat in the middle with my mother, beside a fat woman who smelled of fish. Her bottom was so big it kept pushing me and whenever I wriggled to create space, she would look at me and hiss.

We drove onto a long bridge that snaked over a shimmering mass of water. Somebody behind me was telling a young woman with him that it was the Third Mainland Bridge.

'It's the longest bridge in Africa,' the man said. 'They say it takes four days to walk from one end to the other.'

When I looked up, my mother was peering at the man with an expression that said she didn't believe him. I knew that look. It was the look she had had on her face when her friend came back from Italy and told us how she had married, and divorced, a white man.

Five years have gone by since I arrived in Lagos with my mother on a giddy Saturday afternoon, but I remember that day as if it were yesterday. I remember it the way I can taste the salt on my lips, residue from the corn I have just finished eating.

We got down at Obalende and my mother turned to me and said, 'Hold my hand.'

She said it as if I had done something wrong, but I searched my head and couldn't remember what I had done to make her angry, so I held her hand and walked beside her, breaking into a short run at intervals to keep up.

My mother had been to Lagos before. In fact, she had lived in the city for two full years with an uncle, but he died suddenly, knocked down by a truck as he tried to cross the expressway.

'It was bad luck. The devil really exists, you know. Paulina had made all the plans for us to go to Italy together, and then Uncle Stanley had to go and let a truck kill him. I came to the village with his wife. We were waiting for the mourning period to end when I got pregnant. How can you tell me the devil doesn't work overtime?'

I heard my mother tell this story once to a friend visiting from Jos. Her name was Justina and she had a limp that made it seem like one part of her bum was bigger than the other.

I was sitting behind the door and doing my homework while they spoke. If my mother had seen me, she would have chased me away. That night, after Justina left, I listened to my mother talking to my grandmother as they prepared dinner.

'Mama, see this world is not fair. See Justina with her short leg. When we were in school, nobody thought she would find a husband. See, now she is married with two children and her husband even bought her a car and sent her home with a driver.'

'The cow without a tail,' my grandmother said, turning to look at my mother. 'It is God that chases the flies away on its behalf.'

Justina is dead now. She was killed when Muslims attacked Christians in Jos. They said she was pregnant when she was killed and that the attackers stopped her car, beheaded her driver, ripped her stomach open and kicked the foetus around like a football.

When my mother heard this, she sat down, rested her chin on her hand and stayed that way the whole day, muttering over and over again, 'This devil knows how to work overtime.'

And that was the thought in my head, too, the day my world, as I knew it, came to an end.

The bus we were on got to Marina and my mother stepped down beside me. While we stood there, still trying to find our bearings, the bus roared off, leaving a cloud of acrid white smoke behind. I looked up and the sign atop the long building with fancy blocks in front of it said "General Post Office".

My mother and I crossed the street and, as I walked beside her, she said to me, 'We'll go to Mandilas, so I can buy you some clothes.'

There were rows of shops selling clothes, shoes and belts

and it seemed everyone was talking at the same time.

'Fine girl. Come buy jeans,' someone said, tugging at my mother's arm. I thought she would slap his hand away, but she smiled indulgently and kept walking.

'See. Fine blouse. Wear am go church na so so vision you go dey see,' another man said.

It was a blue blouse with a dragon design embroidered across the front. My mother stopped and asked him how much it cost. I watched as she placed the blouse against her body to see whether it would fit and I wondered why she had stopped to haggle. Was it the promise of visions or the beautifully-rendered design?

My mother bought the blouse and we walked on, stopping at three other shops to buy three shirts, two pairs of jeans and a pair of canvas shoes for me.

'Take the long sleeves,' my mother said, urging me to take a blue, long-sleeved corduroy shirt the shop owner was offering me. 'You will need it when it gets cold at night.'

We made a few other purchases, mostly bras and panties and frilly things for my mother. Then, finally, she asked me to go with her so we could find something to eat.

My mother ordered rice, beans and plantain for me.

Then, while I ate, she gave me some money.

'Hold this money for me,' she said. 'I need to buy something. Wait for me when you finish eating.'

I took the money, nodded, and then went back to my food. That was the last time I saw my mother.

People were milling about, rushing and hurrying in that relentless motion that defines Lagos, while I sat on the steps of the food seller's shop and cried, turning my head from left to right and back again, hoping to see my mother materialise before me and ask why I was crying, before slapping my eyes dry of tears with a sharp: 'You didn't see me and then you start crying? What's wrong with you? You think you are still a baby? Come on, wipe your tears, let's go.'

The way I was feeling then, I wouldn't have minded one of those slaps. A slap would have been far better than being alone in a busy street in Lagos.

But my mother did not appear, and when the shops began to close as darkness fell across the market, I began to shiver from cold and fear. What was I going to do when everyone left and darkness fell? I had no idea.

I pulled out the corduroy top and began to pull it on when, in a moment of startling clarity, the pieces of the puzzle began to fall into place. *Take the long sleeves. You will need it when it gets cold at night.'*

Had she planned it all the while? Had my mother decided, like a desperate goat, to gnaw off the rope that tethered her so she could roam free in Lagos?

I set the bag down and began to skim through its contents. Aside from my clothes and shoes, my mother had left me one thousand naira and a note that had only one word, the final piece of the puzzle: "Sorry!"

That was when I stopped crying. I stood up, dusted the seat of my trousers and set out for the main road. I walked to the post office, crossed to the other side and joined a few men and boys waiting to buy akara.

While I waited for the bean cakes to turn brown, I worked out my plan. I would sleep, wake up the next day and go to Ojota, where I would take a bus home. Once my father saw me without my mother and once I told him the story of my

misadventure in Lagos, he would do something. What it was
he would do, I had no idea.

I paid for my akara with the leftover change from the food
seller's. Then I bought a canned drink and found a spot in a
dark part of a car park to eat.

As I ate, I saw a man chase a young girl past me. He pushed
her against the wall and tugged at her wrapper, which unravelled
like a loose bandage.

'Don't by-force me,' the girl said, laughing as he tried to take
off her panties. Pushing him gently away, she stepped out of
her panties, then turned her back to him. The man bent her
over as he let his trousers fall. I looked away as they became
one, but I couldn't shut out the sounds the girl made.

I finished my food and walked up and down the street. There
were still cars around but by the time I made it back to the post
office, the street was deserted and men and women, whom I
suspected were mad, were lying in front of the building. There
were a few children too, mostly boys, and they were huddled
together and playing a game of Whot.

I found a space a few feet from them and sat down. I took a
shoelace from one of the new shoes my mother had bought
me and tied up my clothes and shoes into a bundle. Then I
put it under my head and fell asleep.

When I woke, the sun was up. I was stretching and yawning
when I realised that the bundle I had kept under my head was
gone. I sprang up, crying in disbelief. I dipped my hands in
my pocket. The one thousand naira had gone, too.

I started screaming, running into the early Sunday morning
and looking for the thief who had stolen my shoes. I found
him by the woman selling akara. He was one of the boys I had
seen the night before and he was wearing one of my new shirts.

'Thief!' I screamed as I got to him. 'Give me my shirt!'

I was reaching out to grab him when his fist connected with my left eye. I fell and then he was kicking and punching me until I was curled up in a ball and screaming at him to stop. He spat and walked away.

I lay there hurting, dusty and sobbing but nobody looked my way. They came, they bought their akara and they walked off, as if I were a piece of rubbish left by the roadside.

'Come,' someone was saying. 'Stand up.'

I opened my right eye. There was a boy, dark, skinny, about my age. He was standing there with his arms outstretched. I took his arm and he pulled me up. Then he led me to a tap at the end of the park.

'Oya, wash your body,' he said, stepping out of his clothes as he spoke. I looked around first to see that no one was looking. Then I did as he did. Scooping water with what was left of an old bucket, I had my first bath outside, right there in the park.

His name was Michael and, after we had showered, he asked me to go with him.

'Are we going to your house?' I asked, hoping to find an adult who would help make sense of all the madness.

'This is my house,' he said, waving expansively. 'I dey live here for Marina.'

'Where your mama?' I asked, also switching to pidgin.

'I no sabi,' he said, stopping in front of a stall to buy a tin of Robb. 'Rub am for your eye. It is swelling too much.'

I thanked him and applied the ointment to my swollen eye.

'See, first thing you must know be dis, this is Lagos and there is no paddy for jungle. You see, you be JJC and I want to take you to a man who will take care of you or else one day you go wake up and somebody don steal your head,' he said, and laughed. 'You go dey pay the man, o, but at least nobody go steal your thing again, you hear?' He stopped so suddenly mid-stride that I bumped into him.

'So, who be dis man?' I asked, as we began walking again.

'Im name na Baba Ejiga and im na Area Father.'

The Area Father, Baba Ejiga had one eye and he was smoking Indian hemp when we got to his shack, nestled under the bridge at the crook where the sea lost the battle to the metal and concrete pillars which propped up the bridge.

'Mikolo, who be dat?' he asked, his one eye darting furiously from me to Michael. It moved so fast that I had difficulty looking away.

'Na JJC. The bobo just land and e never begin shine im eye.'

'Hey, wetin be your name?' Baba Ejiga asked me.

'My name is Daniel,' I answered and he lowered his head and sighed.

'Na Aje-butter you carry come for me,' he said and shook his head. Then he looked up at me and spoke fluent, un-accented English.

'How in God's holy name did you get here and where did that nasty bruise come from?'

Staring at him, at his itinerant eye, the matted hair, the ramshackle shack and the joint in his left hand, I couldn't reconcile the voice with the man.

After I told him I'd been abandoned and the victim of a robbery, Baba Ejiga was silent for a heartbeat. Then, he shook his head and said to Michael, 'Mikolo, this one na bad market, o, very bad market,' he said, as if I was not there.

He raised his joint to his dark lips, drew long and hard, and then held it out to Michael who took it, sucked on it, inhaled, and handed the joint back. I watched in wonder, my mouth hanging open. Michael couldn't have been much older than me.

'Carry this JJC waka. Make you show am way. If anybody worry una, tell dem say this JJC na my person.'

That was how I came to live on Lagos Island under the protection of Baba Ejiga. We slept on the streets, usually outside Baba Ejiga's shack, while he frolicked inside with one of the many women who never seemed to tire of him.

In the day, Michael and I prowled the market looking for women to assist with their purchases. We were mules, young ala-barus who eked out a living from the pittance they let drop. Sometimes we stole from them, pilfering items from what they'd bought. Most times they never noticed, though sometimes an eagle-eyed woman would catch you and bitch-slap you into the gutter.

We were children, so it was easy for people to forgive us, to put it down to hunger or the devil working overtime, as usual. There were many children living rough on the streets of Marina and we marked our turf, sometimes fighting battles for control. The adults let us bloody ourselves while they sat and watched, amused, as we morphed slowly into what they had long become, little devils with fangs for teeth and claws for fingers.

Once in a while, one of the older boys would be caught stealing: a radio from a parked car or a handbag from a woman exiting the bank. Many of us would give chase and when we caught up with the thief, we would descend on him, kicking and punching him until he was down. Then, someone would find a tyre, another would pour petrol and the hapless thief would go up in flames.

And every time I watched that senseless orgy of rage and violence, I would wonder why we were so quick to land that blow and kick out at one of our own, someone we knew and lived with. Was it out of a feeling of betrayal and anger that he'd let himself be caught, thus tarring all of us with the sludge of shame? Was that what fuelled our rage?

Often, we retired early, bathing in the park or running across to the old quayside where we washed in the briny waters of the Atlantic. It wasn't uncommon to come out of the sea and find your clothes gone, hidden away or cast into the sea by another boy you had offended without knowing.

While the other boys laughed, the unlucky one would walk back naked to wherever he kept his change of clothes. We didn't possess too many things. We were light travellers, unsure of what the next minute held, and that was why all we owned we hid in our stomachs. Our stomachs were our treasure houses because they were easy to transport and no one could steal the food you had eaten or the drink you had taken.

We ate well, saving only the little we needed to pay Baba Ejiga or entertain the young girls who flocked to us like flies to shit. I avoided them, but Flora would never let up, always coming to sit by me while I read old magazines I picked up from the streets or bought when I had extra cash. Of all the boys who lived with Baba Ejiga, Michael and I were the only ones who could read.

'You dey fear woman?' Flora would ask me every time I refused to accept the little things she brought me on her way home from hawking on the streets: a loaf of bread, a tin of sardines or condensed milk.

We became friends the day I took ill with malaria and she ran all the way to Obalende to buy me Fansidar and folic acid;

and later in the evening, when I had stopped throwing up, she bought me jollof rice and dodo.

'I know you like jollof rice and dodo,' she said, wiping the sweat off my brow.

We talked. She was from Delta state, like me. Like me, she had never known her father and like me, her mother had left her at an early age, but hers had drowned.

'You know, when a woman drown she will lie face up, but a man will lie face down. That is how you know whether the dead person inside the water is a man or a woman,' she told me in her shaky English.

Once we became friends, Flora spoke English instead of pidgin to me. She lived with her aunt who was married to a warden at the prison quarters in Ikoyi and, once in a while, I would walk with her all the way to Ikoyi and then take a bike back to Marina.

One night as I saw her off to her own block, she pushed me against the wall and kissed me, surprising me by her impulsiveness.

'When are we going to do it?' she asked.

'Do what?' I asked, lowering my gaze as my heart hammered in my chest.

'Do what? Ah ah. Sometimes, I feel that you are fearing woman.'

'But you are not even a woman,' I said.

'Who said? I am thirteen years and Janet is twelve but she is doing it with Michael.'

'Michael is older than me.'

'Ehen, it doesn't matter,' Flora said, and reached for me again.

This time, our kiss lingered and Flora was moaning and I was feeling her breast when someone slapped and punched me. We sprang apart and a huge man started punching and slapping Flora as she ran, and kept calling her a whore.

The next day, when I saw Flora she had a black eye and a cut above her upper lip.

'Na my auntie husband. He was angry because he wants to by-force me and I don't agree,' she told me that night as we sat at the back of the car park and kissed. This time our kisses were long and languorous and gentle because I was careful not to hurt her lips.

'God will punish him,' I said, with impotent rage.

Even though Flora wanted us to, I never summoned up enough courage, so we spent our times together kissing and sometimes, when no one was nearby, she would lift her dress and let me fondle and kiss her small breasts.

Then one day I waited and waited and she didn't come to the Marina. When I still didn't see her after three days, I sought out Janet and asked where Flora was.

'Why u dey ask me, no be u pregnant am?' she snapped at me. Flora was pregnant.

That was when I began to drink.

Without Flora, and with nothing to occupy me in the evenings, I started drowning my sorrows, sitting with other boys and men in front of the women who sold kai-kai, the local brew, drinking my life away.

I didn't smoke cigarettes or hemp because they made me light-headed so I sat there and drank shot after shot of kai-kai. But while everyone else got drunk, I would remain clear-eyed and sure-footed. Soon, my reputation spread and people came to see the eleven-year-old boy who could down a bottle of kai-kai and still walk straight.

Michael was the one who told Baba Ejiga and the one-eyed

man, always eager to make a quick buck, began arranging drinking bouts for me with men who would square up against me and end up being carried away by friends, after they had lost their bearings and their bets.

I never found out what it was that made me incapable of getting drunk, but it made me popular, and the women who sold drinks would offer me free drinks because they knew that my presence at their stalls would attract customers.

But it all ended the day I stole a wallet. This wallet wasn't filled with money but with pictures and cards. A note, scrawled on the back of the picture of a smiling man, read:

"Mummy Rose, you took me from the streets and gave me a new life at Sweet Home. Without you I would be dead now, burnt on the streets like a common thief. But today I am a doctor and even though I do not know what God looks like, when I close my eyes and think of God, I see your face. Love always, Keme."

I would read the note, turn the picture over to look at the smiling face of Keme, and then read the note again. He was tall and big and dressed in convocation garb. Looking at him, I became suddenly dissatisfied with my life. I was like someone coming awake from a bad dream.

'Let's find this woman,' I said to Michael.

'How?' he asked, through a cloud of cigarette smoke. 'See this card. It says "Rose McGowan, Founder, Sweet Home for Boys" and there's an address in Yaba.'

'So, how will you say you got her wallet?' Michael asked. 'I found it on the streets,' I said.

'And?' he asked.

'And I decided to return it to the owner.'

'Dis boy, kai-kai has turned your head. If that woman sees you, she will lock you up.'

'Michael, let's try. Our life can change and we can be like Keme.'

Michael stood up, flung his half-smoked cigarette into the overflowing gutter and exhaled loudly.

'Daniel, too much hope is not good for people like us,' he said and walked away.

I left early the next morning, afraid that dallying would weaken my resolve. I took a bus to Sabo, then got on a bike that took me to Oyadiran estate.

When you pick a pocket or reach into a woman's bag and pick a naira note or wallet or mobile phone, your mind is focused on two things: filching what you can, and not getting caught. You usually don't know what your victim looks like. So when Rose McGowan came to the door after I'd spoken to the maid, I was surprised to see an ageing woman with an American accent.

'Yes, wetin I go do for you?' she asked in pidgin as she took in my shabby appearance.

I didn't speak. I reached into my back pocket as she flinched and took a step back. She relaxed as I pulled out the wallet and extended it to her.

'Where did you find that?' she asked, reaching out to take it.

'Mummy Rose, I am a street boy and I need your help,' I said and then burst into tears.

I wake up and the ceiling is white. There is a ceiling fan and it is whirring slowly. I am sweating and my heart is pounding, but it is not from fear but from excitement. I have been here for months but I still feel like a hungry man who has stumbled on a feast. I still cannot believe that it is all true and real.

I swing my legs off the bed. I find my slippers and walk outside.

The sun is bright. It is a lazy Sunday afternoon and Michael is lying on his back under the almond tree behind the hostel and reading a novel. I sit on the grass beside him and knock the book out of his hands.

'Mikolo!' I say and Michael laughs.

'May his soul rest in peace,' Michael says.

Baba Ejiga died two weeks after I ran away. A jealous husband had surprised him atop his wife and pierced him through the heart with a rusty dagger. This was two months before I went back for Michael.

'After he died, I couldn't stop thinking of what he said when you left,' Michael told me on his first night at Sweet Home for Boys.

'What did he say?'

He said, 'That boy wasn't supposed to be here.' After we buried him, I sat in his shack and for the first time I wondered why I didn't leave with you.'

I am fourteen years old now and I am dying. My liver is ruined, eaten away by all that kai-kai I drank like water in the days when I lived rough.

Michael was supposed to take over my top bunk and the new canvas shoes I got for Christmas, when I die.

But my friend has beaten me to it. Two weeks ago, we buried Michael, the one with the healthy liver, the one who didn't have the angel of death hovering over him.

Now that he is dead, everyone says he knew he was going to die because of the things he did that Saturday afternoon when we all got up to go to the river.

'I'm not going,' Michael had said to me when I tapped him on the chest and roused him from the light sleep he had fallen into as he listened to music on his new MP3 player, the one he got as a prize for coming first in the spelling competition.

'Why?' I asked, pulling the wrapper off him.

'I want to sleep,' he said and tried to grab the wrapper from me, but I was holding on too tight and the wrapper tore.

'See, see. You tore it,' Michael said and jumped off the bed.

I ran but he didn't give chase. He just walked out of the hostel and sat on the dwarf fence that ringed the building, and stared out into the distance as if expecting somebody. I knew he wasn't expecting anybody because no one ever comes to visit.

'Sorry,' I said, touching him, but he brushed off my hand.

'Leave me alone.'

Michael didn't talk to me until we left and he didn't even speak to me when he ran behind us and joined our group. Once or twice on our walk, I would ask a question and look at him, but he would ignore me and stare straight ahead.

'See, the twins of Ikorodu, they are fighting,' someone said and the other boys sniggered.

Michael and I were the closest in the hostel and we never, ever, seemed to fight, so no one could understand why we weren't talking.

When we got to the river and separated into two groups, Michael said he wasn't going to play and just sat on the sand, watching.

When I think about it now, I guess that's why so many people say he knew he was going to die. Everything he did that day was strange. First, he said he didn't want to come. Then, when he did, he said he didn't want to play with us. And then, he didn't want to talk to me.

Michael would still be alive if he had stayed back at the hostel. Or if he had come with us and just sat on the sand like he wanted to. But he didn't. Every time the ball bounced outside the line, Michael would jump up and chase after it. Then, when he got the ball, usually from the river, he would throw it up and spike.

I wasn't looking. I had stubbed the big toe of my left foot and broken my toe nail. I was trying to peel off the broken nail which was still hanging from my toe when I heard my name.

I looked up and all the boys were running to the river bank.

I saw his back, I heard him scream, a watery gurgle more like, and then he was gone, the waves frothing where his red shirt billowed in the rushing water.

The Car They Borrowed

There is blood on the driver's seat.

This is the first thing Bunor notices as he pulls open the door of his new car. A white, blood-stained kaftan is draped over the front passenger's seat. Bunor jumps back in horror. He takes a look at the shimmering black paint. He walks to the back and checks the black sticker his wife gave him two days earlier, the day after he brought the car home. He had liked the legend: *"If God bi fo mi!"*

It is his car. There's no mistake about it.

He circles back to the front and peers in. 'There is a smudge on the seat'. He reaches in a finger and his finger comes up with blood. He wipes it on the steering wheel and stands back to look at his car again. That is when he realises that the engine is running, like they said it would be.

'You will go to Mobil Filling station at 3 o'clock; you know the one on the expressway? Cross to the other side and you will see your car. The engine will be running. Get in and drive home and forget about this meeting.'

Bunor sits up in bed at 5.30am. He hasn't slept well. Like a child with a new toy who can't wait to show it off, he tosses and turns as he thinks of how he will make an entrance at the end-of-year party his village folk hold every year in the city where he lives. He will arrive late to ensure everyone sees him when he lets his wife out of his car before finding a place to park. After years of trundling around town in that old jalopy, he is going to savour his moment of glory. Those who used to laugh at him in the days when his old car would not start are in for a big surprise.

Rolling out of bed, he goes to the bathroom that stands between the children's room and the one he shares with his wife. He lifts the toilet seat and recoils in disgust.

'Martha! Martha!!'

The house help comes running in from the living room where she sleeps, clutching her wrapper to her chest.

'How many times will I tell you to always flush the toilet before you sleep, eh?' he asks, and slaps her with his open palm. The sudden and unexpected blow knocks the girl off her feet and, as she tries to steady herself, her wrapper slips and she is naked before her master. Bunor looks at her full breasts and his eyes widen.

'Oya, flush that thing before I kill you,' he says, standing there and watching as she tries to make herself decent under his gaze.

While he is at his business, his thoughts are still on the house girl. Her ripe nakedness has surprised him. Was it not just yesterday that his wife brought her home, a mere ten-year-old with pimples for breasts? He wonders whether she is still a virgin and just thinking about her makes him grow hard.

Bunor returns to bed with an urgent need. He turns his wife over and pulls off her wrapper.

'Bunor...' she begins to say as he parts her legs and covers her lips with his.

'We need your car for just four hours,' the fat one says, staring straight at Bunor and Bunor can smell ganja on his breath.

He sleeps after making love to his wife. And it is almost daylight when he rises. Bunor picks up his shorts from the floor and walks downstairs, whistling and scratching as he goes.

The landlord's son is washing the landlord's old, weather-beaten 505 saloon, the one he has driven for twelve years.

'Only God knows what he does with the rent he gets from all these houses he owns,' Bunor had said to his wife as they walked upstairs two nights before, after he had gone to ask the landlord to bless his new car for him.

'It's not everyone who likes a fine car,' Angie had replied. 'Remember, he has all those wives and children to take care of.'

'Who told you that? The man doesn't take care of anybody. Four wives and he is still looking outside. And who says people don't like fine cars? Those who say that are the kind of men who marry ugly wives because they don't want other men to look at their wives. Me, I looked well-well before I married you. Who will see this backside and say he wants an ugly woman?' Bunor hit his wife playfully on the backside.

'Bunor,' she remonstrated. 'That's all you know.'

'At least, I know something,' he said and they both laughed.

He had married her straight out of secondary school, after meeting her while on a short visit to see his mother, who had just left hospital.

'Give me grandchildren before I die,' his mother had said.

'Mama, I will,' he said with a sigh, as he settled beside her on the long settee. 'I came to see how you are doing.'

He saw Angie a short while later. Light of build and fair of skin, she pleased him the way a ripe fruit pleases the eyes even before the tongue has known its tangy sweetness.

His mother smiled when her son's eyes lingered on the girl, watching her as she busied herself around the house, washing dishes, making lunch and serving mother and son.

'You say she is Offor's daughter?' Bunor asked for the umpteenth time and his mother smiled to herself, pleased that her son was pleased.

'That's what I said,' she told him, as she dipped her ball of fufu in the soup.

'But how come I never met her before?' Bunor asked, licking his fingers and looking at the young woman from the corner of his eye. His mother's unspoken reply was a knowing smile.

Bunor returned two months later to make Angie his wife before taking her back with him to the city. She made him a happy man, but it was a happiness that brought him anxiety. At home, he loved to watch her walk around his room naked. He loved to gaze upon her mature but innocent beauty but he soon discovered that he was not the only one who liked to look upon his wife. He knew that when other men looked, they also saw what he saw and that knowledge made him sick to the heart, especially since he was only a young man starting out in life. They lived, then, in a one room apartment with a bed, chair and stool for furniture. He didn't own a TV set; there was just a small transistor radio permanently tuned to a station that played Congolese music.

His humble station in life was a source of worry because he knew that a richer man could easily tempt his prize away with money, or the things money could buy, things he could ill afford. And it didn't help, either, that he had married her as a virgin. Bunor lived in mortal fear of Angie being tempted to see if what she was getting at home was the best there was.

When he made his fears known to Uzor, his best friend, Uzor had been quiet for a heartbeat and then said, 'You must test her and then you must beat her.'

'What do you mean, test her? What kind of test?' Bunor asked and Uzor had pulled him close and whispered in his ears.

'Once you do it, she will never try any nonsense.'

That Saturday, Bunor came home earlier than usual and stood outside the door waiting for Angie, who had been to visit an old classmate who had just married and moved to the city.

'Where have you been all day?' he asked, the moment she stepped into the corridor that led to their room.

'I told you I was going to visit Nelly,' she said.

'And you didn't see any other dress to wear?' he asked, looking with disgust at the pink print dress she had on.

'Bunor! But you bought me this dress. Are you sure everything is okay?' she asked and his reply was a slap that cut her lower lip. As she raised her hand to wipe the blood, Bunor pushed her down on the bed, pulled up her dress, tore off her panties and inserted two fingers into her. He pulled his fingers out and then stuck them under his nose.

'God has saved you,' he said and barged out of the room as Angie lay there, shivering.

Even though Angie passed the test, Bunor never let go. He was still susceptible to random attacks of jealousy. Sometimes, they would be at their town's meeting and if he noticed a man looking in her direction, Bunor would turn to her, his face a hideous mask of jealousy and rage.

'Why did you wear that red lipstick, eh? I told you not to wear it. Oya, go and wipe it off.' And like an obedient child,

Angie would rise to do his bidding.

Her calm subservience was not enough. To him, it could well have been a mask for adultery so he took to watching her, paying young boys and girls in their compound and on their street to monitor her and whenever he heard reports about her that suggested something might be amiss, he would beat her, venting his frustration through violence. He was like a man who had stolen a whistle but could not blow it for fear of discovery.

'Who was the man in the red car?' he asked one Saturday night as he walked into their apartment. Bunor had been drinking, as usual, and had just learnt from one of his spies that his wife had been spotted talking to a man in a red car that afternoon.

'What red car?' she asked him, setting down the tray that contained his food on the three-legged stool.

'You know what red car,' he said and slapped her so hard she fell on the stool and overturned the tray. The sight of the wasted food and the accumulated silt of his dark frustrations fuelled his rage and he beat and slapped and kicked her until she was a bleeding and whimpering heap on the floor.

Angie was rushed, bleeding, to the hospital that night.

'If you bring this woman here again, I will report you to the police, you hear me?' the doctor said to Bunor inside his office. 'If you do not want her in your house, send her home. She is somebody's child, you know.'

'I am sorry, doctor,' Bunor said, standing there like a naughty school boy summoned to the staff room.

'You better be,' the doctor said, flopping into a seat. 'I'm sure you know we have to keep her here. She just had a miscarriage.'

The doctor's words were like a whip on his bare skin and

Bunor's eyes watered with tears.

'Doctor, what did you just say?'

'I said you just kicked your child out of her womb and you are lucky I am not calling the police.'

That was the last time Bunor laid a finger on his wife.

'Give us the car keys,' the one with the full moustache says to Bunor, a gun appearing as if by magic in his hand. 'We just need to borrow it for a while.'

Bunor is listening but really not hearing him. His mind is on the whiff of marijuana floating in the air between them.

Bunor is nineteen and formal education as he knows it has just come to an end. He has received his secondary school leaving certificate and is out celebrating with his friends. They have borrowed two cars from two sets of well-to-do parents and gone for a picnic.

Bongos Ikwe's voice is issuing out of loudspeakers. His deep voice is singing 'What's gonna be is gonna be, there's nothing to do about it,' and the young men and women are echoing the words, aware that the cushioned life is over. Now, they must stare life eyeball to eyeball as young adults.

Bunor is sitting away from the group. A joint is burning between his fingers, its thick smoke pluming into the air. His mind is on his impending trip to Lagos where he is to join his uncle's business, effectively ending his dream of university education. He always knew secondary school would be all his parents could afford but now that it has come to pass, Bunor feels the loss keenly.

He watches his friends as they sing and dance and scream. There is food and drink aplenty and everyone is in a happy mood. He watches the girls. Some will get pregnant this evening, after the drink and food are gone and boys and girls couple like dogs on heat. In a year, there will be babies for those who don't abort the pregnancies.

Some of his friends, those whose parents can afford it, will go on to university while the rest will get married and live out their lives in the provincial ambience of the village, their dreams turning to cobwebs as they slowly become all they hate in their parents.

Bunor takes a drag on the joint, flings it away and rises to his feet.

'What's gonna be is gonna be, there's nothing to do about it,' he sings as he joins his friends in the revelry.

'Don't go to the police, you hear me?' the fat guy says as he slides behind the steering wheel. 'We are not stealing your car, we are just borrowing it for a few hours.

'When you pick it up, check under the passenger seat. There'll be something there for you. Then, drive it straight home. Don't go to the police because we will be watching you,' the moustachioed guy says as he gets into the passenger seat.

Bunor climbs the stairs and walks like a zombie into the bedroom, without acknowledging his wife and children.

'If I had known, I would have washed the car in the compound,' he says to himself, not realising he has spoken out loud.

'What's wrong with washing it outside?' his wife asks and he bursts into tears.

'Bunor, what's wrong? Did something happen?' Angie kneels and cradles his tearful face in her hands.

'They took the car.'

'Who took the car?' she asks, and not waiting for an answer, runs to the window. She looks outside and a dry patch surrounded by wet ground is the only evidence that a car had been parked there. She screams.

'Bunor, who took our car?'

After Bunor has mastered his emotions and tells her the story, she says they must let the police know.

'But they warned me not to. They said they were just borrowing it.'

'And you believe them. They don't want you to go to the police so that by the time you finally make a report, the car will be far gone. We have to report it, o.'

'Angie, they said four hours. Let us wait.'

'In four hours, the car could be in Onitsha,' she says. 'Okay, if you don't want to make a formal report, let's go and see Nelly's husband. You know he is a policeman.'

Nelly's husband, Ikenna, fat and big-bellied like most police officers, is picking his teeth when they enter.

'Beer or stout?' he asks, as Bunor settles into a seat andAngie disappears into the kitchen where her friend is doing the dishes.

'Nothing for now. I have come with a big problem.'

'Then you've come to the right place. The police is your friend, you know,' he says, laughing.

'So, what is the problem?'

Bunor tells him what has happened and about the warning. When he is done, Nelly's husband is snoring gently, the toothpick bobbing between his quivering lips.

'Ikenna!' Bunor screams and the fat man jumps.

'Sorry, my brother,' Ikenna says. 'I came back this morning

from a useless night patrol. Anyway, they gave you the right advice and you should obey it. Don't make a police report. No need for that. Just go where they asked you to and pick up your car. If it's not there you can call me. Go home and rest.'

Bunor exchanges looks with his wife who has rejoined them.

'You say I shouldn't make a report?'

'Ehen, that's what I said. Go and pick up your car like they asked you to, and thank your God.'

'3 o'clock. Don't be late they o!' the moustachioed guy says as he zooms off.

When he realises that the engine is running like they said it would be, Bunor reaches under the passenger's seat and fingers a bag. He pulls out the bag and inside are wads of hundred naira notes. He pushes the bag back, looks around to see whether anyone is watching, gets in behind the wheel and slips the gearstick into Drive.

'There is a bloodstained kaftan and money in the car,' his wife is saying to him. 'Maybe they killed somebody and somebody could have got the car number. Go and make a report. Tell them the car was stolen and now has been returned. You don't have to talk about the money.'

Bunor tells her to hush but she persists until, worn out, he asks her to come with him to the police station. When they get there, he asks her to wait in the car.

It is dusk and the station is busy. Wives, siblings and friends of the detained are massed outside bearing food, changes of clothing, medicine and other essentials. Bunor pushes through until he gets to the counter, where three policemen are seated.

'Good evening,' he begins. 'I...'

The uniformed officer sitting in front of him is the moustachioed man who borrowed his car earlier in the day. He looks at Bunor with eyes that have narrowed into angry slits.

'Didn't I tell you to stay at home?' he hisses. 'Didn't I tell you to take what we left for you and go home?' Bunor stares, unable to speak.

'Get out of here!' the man barks and Bunor is startled, but still he doesn't move because there is a puddle at his feet and his trousers are wet and warm and clinging to his legs.

Sad Eyes

She had sad eyes with a face that was made for crying. But you knew at once she was a girl who had taught herself not to cry.

Stella had a look that made you feel guilty even when you had done nothing wrong. She was like an open door to your conscience.

I met Stella when I was young and carefree. I had just found a job that paid well, and even though she was a pretty girl who made my mind bubble with naughty thoughts, I doused my desire with a basinful of selfishness.

My answer was "no" to a question I didn't dare ask. I knew that if I let myself go, I'd fall truly, madly and deeply for her. So I steeled my heart like a Spartan's. And Stella knew, and did nothing, and it was this nothing she did that made me sick with guilt: that look she gave me which, though silent, levelled a million charges against me.

We met on the creaky, half-lit staircase of our computer school. I was late. She was early and we were both going in opposite directions.

'Shit!' I said, as the lights went off.

'Oh!' she cried, disappointment colouring her voice.

'Hold on. There's someone here,' I mumbled, waving a hand in front of me like a roach's antenna. It fell on one of her breasts and I withdrew it immediately.

'I'm sorry,' I said.

'Why? Haven't you touched a woman's breast before?'

'Well...em...' I stuttered.

'I embarrassed you, abi? Okay, tell me. Are you wearing a red tie and a white shirt today?'

'What?' I asked, a funny feeling creeping up inside me.

'You heard me.' She had a rumour of laughter in her voice.

'Who are you?" I asked, stepping back.

'Stella. And you?'

'You know me. You know what I wear and you can see in the dark.'

'Yes, but not your name.'

'Osa,' I told her.

'You're Bendel?'

'Edo,' I corrected.

'Same thing. So, about the tie?'

'Yes. It's a shade of red,' I admitted.

The staircase was dark, stuffy and low. Whoever built it was short and didn't care. My first week there, I bumped my head four times.

'You're moving back,' she said, her voice staying my feet.

'How do you know?'

'If you keep your focus you can see in the dark.'

'How?'

'By focusing.' She laughed a deep, throaty laugh that belonged to a man.

'I laugh like a man,' she said gauging my thoughts. 'Alright.' My pen was ready to stab out if she approached me.

'Put down your pen. You might hurt me,' she said and swept past me.

I followed, crouching low, as I gobbled up the steps with feet made ravenous by curiosity. I burst out downstairs and she was there, smiling.

'Hi,' she said, her smile spreading. A ray of light from a generator fell directly on her face.

'It was spooky up there,' I said.

'I didn't mean to scare you.'

'How can you see in the dark?'

'I concentrate.'

'On what?'

'The dark. Once you do that, everything else takes shape.'

I relaxed a bit and leaned on the fence and she said, 'Take care. There could be scorpions.'

'Yeah, in Lagos,' I mocked.

'I killed one yesterday and I'll kill one tonight. Stay still.' Then she reached out, flicked something off my shirt and stepped on it.

'What was that?' I asked, my mouth going dry.

'A scorpion. Here, take a look.'

I looked. The scorpion's upper body was crushed but its tail still moved.

'How did you know?' I asked, fear nibbling at the edges of my mind.

'I can smell snakes and scorpions.'

'What else can you do?'

'I can tell colours with my fingers.'

She could do all these things and much more but she could not raise enough money to pay her fees. We were taking a computer appreciation course. A few days after our strange encounter, she walked out before our Excel test and I followed her.

'Why are you out here?' I asked.

'Go and write your test,' she said, her eyes hooded behind long and thick eyelashes.

'I will, but why are you here?'

'A few things are better left untold,' she said, but I prised words out of her like a miner feeling in the muck to find the nuggets nestling within.

I paid her fees and learned that she was head of a home, the only girl in a family of four. Her parents' death had made her father and mother to three younger brothers.

'I work. I earn money but it's never enough. My brothers fall sick, break neighbours' louvres and sprain their ankles when they play ball. I need help but I don't know where to find it,' she told me one night in a restaurant.

'You don't have a boyfriend?'

'I've had a couple. But they get scared when they learn of my burden. You don't have a girlfriend. She left you,' she said.

'How do you know?'

'You wear it on your sleeve. Your pain is raw. Let it heal.'

'How?'

'Learn to love again.'

I took her advice. I found love again. But I did not choose Stella.

Now, chastened by a new and terrible knowledge, I ask myself, 'Why didn't I?'

She made you think of marriage the moment you set eyes on her, but how could I marry her and three others? I was young. I had a brother to see through school and a life to live. I wasn't ready to be weighed down with excess baggage. So one night, after we got back from the hospital where doctors had stitched her brother's cut, I fled. The boy had a nasty wound

and had lost a lot of blood. I helped carry him to the only bed
in the room and then, after we had made him comfortable, I
told her I had to leave.

Tears stood in her eyes as she said thanks. 'Here.' I offered
her a wad of notes.

'You've done enough,' she said, refusing the money.

'Take it. You'll need it.' I swallowed back the lump that rose
to my throat.

'Don't talk about need,' she said, forcing herself not to cry. I
let the money drop as I walked to the car, kicked it, and drove
off. I left that night and never went back.

In the six months we'd been friends, she'd made no demands.
She had taken what I had offered and thanked me. She had
never asked to know my place, even though she took me to her
own home, a small, one-room affair that was poor but clean.

Two nights ago, I ran into her brother as I drove my wife
and infant son home from the hospital.

'How is Stella?' I asked, wondering at the lines tough life
had etched on his young face.

'She died two years ago. She was found in a ditch. Her private
parts gone.'

The Phone Call Goodnight

The phone rang. I did not pick it up.

I knew who was calling: my husband. He was on his way
home, five minutes away actually, and he was calling to let me
know so I could ask the house help to go and open the gate
for him. That was our routine.

'Fidelia!' I called out as I depressed the mute button on the
remote control to get the volume of the television set down.
'Oya, go and open the gate for Uncle,' I said, without even
looking at her as I went back to watching *Desperate Housewives*.

Then my phone rang again. I reached for the remote control
and handset both at once. The caller ID told me it was my
husband. I pressed MUTE with my left hand and then pressed
ANSWER with my right.

'Yes,' I said, with all the sauciness I could muster. He must
have met a friend or neighbour and was calling me to ask the
house help to wait.

'Pray for ...' I heard my husband say, then I heard him scream.

'Ndu! Ndu!' I screamed, but there was no answer. There
were voices now. Loud and angry voices. And my husband
was begging.

'Please, please. I have money in the boot. Please don't hurt
me.'

'Shut up,' a voice said. Then I heard a slap and my husband's voice saying, 'Take it easy, please.'

There was another slap and someone was saying, 'Move to the back seat. Move. Now!'

It was all happening too fast. One minute I was watching Eva Longoria and awaiting my husband's return. The next minute everything had changed and I was in a nightmare world.

I heard screeching tyres; then there was silence, but this silence wasn't the absence of sound, it was the silence of amplified fear, of raw and primal fear manifested as panting, the deep wheezing kind of breathing that spells fear in capital letters.

Holding my phone to my ear, I ran downstairs without my slippers. The gate was wide open and the house help was standing there, her left hand shielding her eyes as she peered into the distance to see whether Ndu's car was coming.

I ran past her, out into the road and looked. There was no car. 'Did you see Uncle's car?' I asked, panting.

'Yes. I saw him talking to three men; then they just turned and went back. I am waiting for him.'

The night was suddenly alive with danger. My husband was still panting in my ear. I could hear his fear, smell it, just like I could smell the acrid odour of burning rubber that still hung in the air.

As I stood with Fidelia at the gate, I heard my husband's voice again.

'Pally, I said I have money in the boot. It's over sixty thousand naira. You can take it with the car. Please let me drop here, I...' He didn't finish the sentence before I heard him cry out and then he was groaning.

'I told you before. SHUT UP!' That was when I began to cry. When Ndu left the house that morning, we hadn't kissed each other goodbye. I had been angry with him from the night before.

'Do not let the sun go down on your anger,' he had said, sing-songy in the bathroom as he showered in readiness for work. I ignored him and concentrated on getting the children ready for school.

Our quarrel was silly but one you can appreciate if you are us. I was not exactly angry. What I needed was attention. Ndu had been busy on a project and had forgotten to pick up a pair of shoes his colleague had found for me. With size 43 feet, buying shoes can be a nightmare. So, whenever I see a pair that fits, I snatch them up. Ndu's colleague, thinking I didn't want them anymore, had sold the shoes to someone else. I was still sulking.

'I will pay for two,' Ndu told me as he tried to slip his hand underneath my short nightgown when we were in bed.

'Stop,' I said, mock-seriously, slapping his hand away.

'Give a man some,' he said, as his palm covered my left breast.

'Stop it or I'll go to the children's room.'

'Ok, if that's what you want, but I thought we could talk about this without fighting,' Ndu said, a trace of anger creeping into his voice. 'I've told you I will buy you two pairs. Don't worry yourself about how I am going to find them.'

Ndu waited for me to say something, to signal that it was okay, that we could go on and make love, but I just lay there breathing evenly, my back turned to him.

I heard his loud exhalation of air and then he patted his pillows and slept.

I was up before him the next day and I was laying out the children's lunch packs in the kitchen when he came and grabbed me from the back and I felt his hardness digging into my buttocks.

'The kids will be late,' I said, pushing him away.

'Let them be,' he said, reaching for me again.

'Then we'll have to pay a fine,' I said, zipping up their backpacks.

'I'll pay,' Ndu said, but I pushed him away and went to see to the children who were in the bathroom with the house help.

When I came back, he was in the shower and pretending to sing in his husky voice. I hid behind the closet door and laughed softly.

'Take the left turn. LEFT!' a voice snapped. 'There's a police checkpoint in front.'

There was silence for a while and then I heard Ndu's voice pleading and telling them again that he had money in the boot.

'This man, we heard you before. If we want the money we will take it. Just keep quiet and let us do our job.'

There was that same silence again, the one that did not exclude sound but was a diminution of sound and the amplification of fear.

In Igbo language, we call it Osondu: the race for one's life. In English that would translate to "fight or flight". That night, as I stood outside our gate, my phone to my ear, my eyes scanning the road for signs of a car I knew was not there, I felt my heart pumping, the blood roaring in my ears, thoughts of fight and flight buzzing in my head.

Rushing up the stairs, I grabbed my car keys off the dining table and, telling Fidelia to take care of the house, I dashed downstairs, got into my car and, tyres screeching, roared off in search of my husband.

'Madam, how pikin?' one of the guards at the estate gate said to me as I passed, but I was too far gone to reply.

I didn't know where I was going or what I wanted to do. All I knew was that I was in distress and I wanted to find my husband.

As I drove, with one hand on the steering wheel and the other clutching the phone to my ear, I almost ran into an oncoming car. I put the phone on speaker and then, with two hands on the steering wheel, started to retrace the route my husband takes on his way home from work.

All the time, I kept my ear cocked for sound, any sound at all. At that point, with my heart hammering and constricting from fear, even a slap and a cry of pain from my husband would have been welcome. Any sound, no matter how heart rending, would have been like a sliver of light in the dark and a pointer to hope that my husband was still alive and not pushed out of the car and dead some place we'd never find him.

But the more I listened, the more I heard a voice that was not my husband's. The voice in my ear was from years ago, twenty-six years actually, and it was the voice of my mother. I remembered it so clearly because my heart had been pounding from fear and intimations of dreadful things the day I heard it.

I was six and my mum and I had gone to the wedding of a distant relative. Was it a man or a woman? I can't remember. All the details have been swallowed up by the yawning mouth of time. What I remember is that my mother hadn't wanted me to go along, since my father had decided to stay behind because his favourite team was playing.

'Take her, please, and let me have some peace,' my father said, gazing at the television as he watched a football match with Diali, my older brother.

I was bawling and following my mother from the bedroom to the kitchen and begging her to take me, while she tried to shoo me away without success. My mother was angry but it

was not at me. It was at my father, who had suddenly changed
the plan for the weekend. My mother finally relented, gave me
a quick bath and dressed me up in the dress she'd just made
me for Diali's ninth birthday.

All the way, as we drove to the wedding, my mother kept
telling me to behave myself.

'Sit down o, or I will take you home. I don't want you disturbing
me,' she kept saying. By the time we got there, I was already
wondering why I'd ever wanted to go with her.

The venue was a huge hall and I was awed by the enormous
mass of gaily-dressed people. The women were decked in
shimmering lace and brocade with headgears that seemed to
reach into the sky. I stared and stumbled and was glad that
my tiny hand was clutched inside my mother's sweaty palm.

It was a rich and lavish wedding, I remember that. I remember,
also, the food and the soft, fried pieces of meat my mother kept
passing to me. Then suddenly I was sitting at the table all by
myself. I looked up and my mother wasn't there. All around
me were brightly-dressed women with skyscraper headgears.
Enveloped by a sense of panic, I rose and went in search of
my mother.

The more I searched, the more my panic rose. I was crying
and snivelling, and I must have wandered right out of our
own hall and into another, because when I tried to retrace my
steps, I ended up at a table that was draped in gold and black,
instead of the pink and blue that had covered ours.

I was sobbing furiously when I heard the voice. It was strange
and loud and intoning my name.

'Onyinye!'

It was my mother's voice but there was an edge to it, a desperate
timbre. I listened and I could tell, even in my confused and

panic-stricken state, that it was coming from loudspeakers.

'Onyinye! Onyinye!! Onyinye!!! O God, please has anyone seen my daughter? Please God.'

I was trying to get to the speakers but there was a nest of legs like something woven by very industrious birds. Finally, I tugged at a woman's wrapper and she took one look at my face and knew.

'She's here! See her here!' she screamed, scooping me into her bosom and beating a path through the throng to my mother. My mother was crying, too. I remember that. I remember also that she was bare-footed, her headgear was gone and her hair was dishevelled, while her make-up was ruined by her tears.

'Onyi!' she cried, snatching me from the woman who had found me.

She was quiet all the way home and when we got home and I asked her where she had put her shoes and headgear, my mother sighed.

'I threw them away.'

'Why?' I asked.

'Because they were too heavy.'

I was feeling like that young girl as I drove into the darkness in search of my husband and ever since, many people have asked me why I dashed out of the estate into the dark night and onto the long road instead of waiting, or calling for help. 'What did you think you would find?' they ask.

My answer is always a simple one. I needed to be sure. But when they ask what I needed to be so sure of, I find that I am not sure what it was I set out to find. All I know is that something inside me was like a compass pointing me down the dark road.

As I drove, I still strained my ears to listen but I heard nothing.

The phone had either gone dead or been discovered. Yet still I drove on, something telling me to go to the Third Mainland Bridge after I took a left turn to avoid the police checkpoint in front.

I drove slowly on the dark and unlit bridge, my car headlights shining in front of me, my heart hammering as my mouth moved in wordless prayer. I was in the middle of the road and would have missed him but for a speeding car that seemed to come out of nowhere. I swerved to the right as the oncoming car's headlights lit up the interior of my car, and I was straightening up when, in the wing mirror, I saw somebody waving frantically. I stopped and reversed.

What I saw next made me laugh and weep at once. There was a naked man on the bridge, his fingers covering his crotch. I squinted in the dark to see better and who was standing there but Ndu, his face puffy and bloodied.

Acknowledgements

Writing is an intensely personal experience.

But reading, on the other hand, and the very act of book making and promotion and selling and reading can become not just collaborative but very public.

Thank you Bibi, Emma, Kofo, Lynette, Layla and all the other unseen hands tugging at the strings behind the scenes at Cassava Republic.

A special thank you to the journalists and book reviewers and bloggers, book clubs and magazine owners who help push and put our works out there.

Thank you Saraba for publishing 'Strangers' and AGNI for publishing 'The Harbinger'. The other stories appeared, in slightly different forms, in the following journals and newspapers: Drum, Voices Revue, ThisDay, Post Express literary series, Sunday Sun Revue, Daily Independent and webzines like Farafina and Africawriting.com. Others have appeared in anthologies such as Little Drops, Ashes and Diamonds, We-men and Inkwells.

Finally, a big thanks to my father whose library was my first true contact with books and reading.

Awele, Chuka and Ify - love always from Daddy.

Better Never Than Late
Chika Unigwe

ISBN: 978-1-911115-54-0
Nigeria/UK Publication Date: 3rd September 2018
US/Canada Publication Date: Spring 2020

Better Never Than Late charts the unconventional lives and love affairs of a group of Nigerian migrants, making their way in Belgium. The collection is centred around Prosperous and her husband Agu, and the various visitors who gather at their apartment each week. These interconnected stories explore their struggles and triumphs, from unhappy marriages (of convenience or otherwise), to the pain of homesickness, and the tragic paradox in longing to leave Nigeria so that you may one day return to it.

The Whispering Trees
Abubakar Adam Ibrahim

ISBN: 978-1-911115-86-1
Nigeria/UK Publication Date: 8th October 2018
US/Canada Publication Date: Spring 2020

The magical tales in *The Whispering Trees* capture the essence of life, death and coincidence in Northern Nigeria. Myth and reality intertwine in stories featuring political agitators, newly-wedded widows, and the tormented whirlwind, Kyakkyawa. The two medicine men of Mazade battle against their egos, an epidemic and an enigmatic witch. And who is Okhiwo, whose arrival is heralded by a pair of little white butterflies?

Support *Nights of The Creaking Bed*

We hope you enjoyed reading this book. It was brought to you by Cassava Republic Press, an award-winning independent publisher based in Abuja and London. If you think more people should read this book, here's how you can help:

Recommend it. Don't keep the enjoyment of this book to yourself; tell everyone you know. Spread the word to your friends and family.

Review, review review. Your opinion is powerful and a positive review from you can generate new sales. Spare a minute to leave a short review on Amazon, GoodReads, Wordery, our website and other book buying sites.

Join the conversation. Hearing somebody you trust talk about a book with passion and excitement is one of the most powerful ways to get people to engage with it. If you like this book, talk about it, Facebook it, Tweet it, Blog it, Instagram it. Take pictures of the book and quote or highlight from your favourite passage. You could even add a link so others know where to purchase the book from.

Buy the book as gifts for others. Buying a gift is a regular activity for most of us – birthdays, anniversaries, holidays, special days or just a nice present for a loved one for no reason... If you love this book and you think it might resonate with others, then please buy extra copies!

Get your local bookshop or library to stock it. Sometimes bookshops and libraries only order books that they have heard about. If you loved this book, why not ask your librarian or bookshop to order it in. If enough people request a title, the bookshop or library will take note and will order a few copies for their shelves.

Recommend a book to your book club. Persuade your book club to read this book and discuss what you enjoy about the book in the company of others. This is a wonderful way to share what you like and help to boost the sales and popularity of this book. You can also join our online book club on Facebook at Afri-Lit Club to discuss books by other African writers.

Attend a book reading. There are lots of opportunities to hear writers talk about their work. Support them by attending their book events. Get your friends, colleagues and families to a reading and show an author your support.

Thank you!

Stay up to date with the latest books, special offers and exclusive content with our monthly newsletter.
Sign up on our website:
www.cassavarepublic.biz

Twitter: @cassavarepublic #ReadCassava #ReadingAfrica
Instagram: @cassavarepublicpress
Facebook: facebook.com/CassavaRepublic

Transforming a manuscript into the book you are now reading is a team effort. Cassava Republic Press would like to thank everyone who helped in the production of *Nights of the Creaking Bed*:

Editorial
Bibi Bakare-Yusuf
Layla Mohamed

Design & Production
Seyi Adegoke
Tobi Ajiboye

Sales & Marketing
Emma Shercliff
Kofo Okunola

Publicity
Lynette Lisk
Nikki Mander